LIFE ALMOST STILL

Life Almost Still

ANTHEM PRESS
An imprint of Wimbledon Publishing Company Limited (WPC)
First published in the United Kingdom in 2016 by
ANTHEM PRESS
75–76 Blackfriars Road
London SE1 8HA

www.anthempress.com

Natura quasi morta
Copyright © Carme Riera, 2011
Edicions 62, S.A. Avda. Diagonal 662-664, 08034 Barcelona
English translation copyright © Josep Miquel Sobrer, 2011

The translation of this work was supported by a grant from the
Institut Ramon Llull.

A CIP record for this book is available from the British Library.

ISBN 978–1–78308–461–6

This title is also available as an ebook.

LIFE ALMOST STILL

Carme Riera

Translated from the Catalan by
Josep Miquel Sobrer

ANTHEM PRESS

To Lluna, our dog, in memoriam

Author's Note

On 13th November 2007, between Barcelona and Sabadell, the Erasmus scholarship student Romain Lannuzel disappeared. He has not been heard of since. This novel, which also begins with a disappearance, serves as a reminder that the Lannuzel case remains unsolved.

I want to acknowledge two masters: Francisco González Ledesma for his advice, and Andreu Martín for his constant help and for the detailed reading of a draft of this book.

★

The campus of the Universitat Autònoma de Barcelona (UAB), occupying about 650 acres – 568 acres of which are green spaces – abuts to the north on Bellaterra, to the south on Cerdanyola del Vallès (to whose municipality it belongs), to the east on Badia del Vallès and Sabadell and to the west on Sant Cugat del Vallès and again on Bellaterra. Criss-crossed by 21 kilometres of pathways and three axes, northern, central and southern, the university accommodates 40,000 students, 3,688 professors and 2,340 instructors, plus the administrative and service personnel.

It is a 'Campus of Excellence', the only one in Catalonia, consisting of 57 schools or departments, and it is dedicated to vigorous research. As its assures us, UAB is a privileged spot for students to live in and study. In its Vila, 600 apartments can lodge more than 2,000 people who can easily access shops, cafés, restaurants and the Serhs, a hotel set in a unique environment surrounded by nature.

The *Facultat* or School of Philosophy and Letters, where a good part of this novel takes place, sits on the southeast part of the campus, near the Humanities Library, and shares Building B with the *facultats* of Psychology and Economics. The path leading from the Letters parking lot to Ciutat Badia via a small wooded area after crossing highway C-58 through a tunnel is an important setting for our story. The same goes for the rectorate or administration building, the apartments of the Vila and the Serhs to its northwest. You can get to the school from the parking lot after a short walk or you can hop on the bus that serves the campus as Laura Cremona and Domenica Arrigo, important characters in this narrative, used to do.

If you are interested in visiting the Bellaterra Campus, as it is often called, you can get there from Barcelona by several means. A very sustainable one – and the one preferred by Professor Bellpuig and Marcel Bru, the two protagonists of this novel – is the Ferrocarrils de la Generalitat train line, which stops at the UAB itself or the national railroad line, RENFE, which entails getting off at Cerdanyola and then taking a bus. If you drive, you can choose between three highways: AP-7, C-58 or B-1414.

In the UAB libraries, open on quite a generous schedule, you will find more than a million books, and the adjacent lawns are a most pleasant spot for a breath of fresh air. If you pay attention, you might get a whiff of science, critical spirit and innovative knowledge which are the backbone of the university's mission.

All the places mentioned above are in the *comarca* (something akin to a US county) of El Vallès, within the Spanish autonomous region of Catalonia whose capital Barcelona lends its name to the university and where a good number of students and faculty live. The main cities within El Vallès are Terrassa and Sabadell. Halfway between these, the Catalan autonomous police, the Mossos d'Esquadra ("Squad Boys"), have *its center* of operations, the Complex Egara. The *mossos* are the police body in charge of the investigations in this novel.

A profusion of flyers bearing the picture of Constantinu Iliescu were pasted on the walls of the different schools. They appeared at the train stations in Bellaterra and Cerdanyola, on the campus buses, in cafés, libraries and the lobbies of the Vila apartments. Flyers also showed up, though not quite as profusely, on the façades of some buildings near Cinema Verdi in the Gràcia neighborhood of Barcelona and on the stairs of the metro stations of Fontana and Lesseps.

The flyers on letter-size paper – it was obvious they were homemade – had a photograph of Iliescu and some personal data: a Romanian student, 21 years old, 5' 9", stocky build, shaven head, blue eyes. Beneath these references, in gigantic capitals, was the word: "DISAPPEARED." Informers were to call the phone numbers printed at the bottom.

These flyers were created by two friends of Iliescu's: Laura Cremona, the Italian girl who was waiting for him the day he vanished, and Marcel Bru, one of Laura's few friends who was not an Erasmus scholarship student. Both Laura and Marcel kept their cell phones switched on day and night in the hope of receiving a clue to Iliescu's whereabouts.

There were many calls. Some merely inquired whether there would be a reward for whoever could offer a lead. Others, in blatant bad taste, came from idle idiots eager to poke fun. There were even some from xenophobes who claimed they were happy Catalonia had one less immigrant. Some called and hung up without a word which really annoyed Laura and Bru who expected to hear a ransom demand or at least get some information that would throw light on the matter Only two calls dealt with the issue in a direct way, both to Laura's cell phone, and they came from phone numbers with the prefix of the Universitat Autònoma de Barcelona where Iliescu, Cremona and Bru were all enrolled.

The first call was from Professor Rosa Casasaies, the adviser to the Erasmus students in the School of Letters, expressing dismay at not having been informed of Iliescu's disappearance before it was made public, especially in such an overwhelming and probably useless display. In those days, the school was almost empty due to strikes. Casasaies was annoyed but made an effort to be kind. Not being able to place Laura by her name, she insisted on knowing what courses Laura had registered for. She wanted to make sure the affair was for real, not a macabre joke that someone was playing on the Romanian student. After all, the school had been occupied by a sit-in protest against the new Bologna legislation for university studies, and for at least one week and a half, the general ruckus had plunged the university into chaos.

From their conversation, Casasaies was convinced that Cremona was telling the truth and had a justifiable reason for not having asked the adviser for help as she had assumed the university would not want to get involved in Iliescu's disappearance. The registrar's office where the students had sought to consult their friend's transcript had refused them the information. They claimed nobody but the student himself could access those private documents, even though all his friends wanted to know was where he stayed when he arrived in Barcelona and his parent's address so they could contact them.

"And from this you get that the university would just wash its hands of the matter?" Casasaies asked with a perplexed inflection in her voice, considering once again the tendency of the young to confuse things. It was one thing for the registrar to have strict orders not to disclose transcripts, but why would academic authorities ignore a student's disappearance?

She got no answer. The professor took advantage of the silence and insisted on the fact that the situation seemed absurd to her. Of course, they had the right to look for their friend, but it was better to act in collaboration with the faculty. To take the frying pan by the handle in a unilateral way, she added, would lead them nowhere.

"Do you understand what I'm saying, Laura?" She asked, attempting to establish a certain complicity by using the student's first name. "Did you understand? Do you know the Catalan idiom 'to take the frying pan by its handle'?"

"I do not," Laura replied drily. "I still haven't learned all the idioms..." Now her voice sounded less arrogant and showed her Italian accent. "What we want is to find Constantinu," she continued, "as soon as possible. If you can help us, all the better."

"Of course, we want to help. How long has it been since you last heard from him?"

"He disappeared six days ago. We waited four days before putting up the flyers," she said in a tearful voice.

"Please come to my office and you can tell me everything calmly," Casasaies proposed.

"I can't go to your office because I'm not in Bellaterra," Laura said, recovering her blunt and aggressive tone which the professor pretended not to hear.

"Come on, honey," Casasaies encouraged her. "You'll see that everything will be all right. I will speak to the dean right away. We'll get in touch with Iliescu's family and you can come by tomorrow morning. I have office hours from eleven to one o'clock. Do you know where my office is?"

★

Rosa Casasaies had long been a professor at the School of Letters. When she started, her students could have been her siblings. She still went out to dinner once in a while with some of her initial students and a few of them had become close friends. In contrast, she had trouble understanding today's students who by their age could be her children; in fact Cristina, her daughter, was twenty. She didn't get along great with Cristina either, despite her efforts to make life at home bearable. She often had to pacify her husband who thought their daughter was a fool, spoilt by her mother right from the start. Spoiled and egoistical, she had built around herself a kind of wall. It was the same wall Rosa sensed in her conversation with Laura Cremona which made her think that communication with the Erasmus students was a sinking ship. But why? What had the school done wrong? It looked like the orientation sessions and the pep talks by the academic authorities telling them to feel at home and not hesitate to ask their advisers for anything they needed had been a waste of time.

The second call, barely an hour after Casasaies', was much shorter. It came from the dean's secretary. The dean was calling a meeting of the Erasmus students and advisers to discuss the measures to take regarding Iliescu's disappearance. The meeting was set for the next day at ten o' clock in the morning in the dean's office.

When Rosa Casasaies informed the dean of her conversation with Laura Cremona, the dean told her that she had just learned of Iliescu's disappearance. It was Professor Bellpuig who, running into her in a hallway, had mentioned the case; he was curious because the Erasmus kid was one of his students.

The dean had not noticed the flyers even though they'd been up for two days.

For more than a week, Dolors Adrover had walked from the parking lot to her office, intent on looking straight ahead. She did not want to see the graffiti related to the new order demanded by the strikers or the banners with insults to the president and to herself under portraits of Hitler and Franco – a clear accusation of fascism.

Being herself a vocal opponent of the Franco regime, Adrover, whose parents had been loyal supporters of the Republic and suffered retaliation under Franco, could not quite fathom by what strange and perverted fashion the kids who had occupied the school could be oblivious to her record as one who had fought hard for democracy and freedom. Worried and depressed, she slept badly, ate poorly and could not concentrate; she considered Iliescu's disappearance an incident of no importance. For about two weeks, since the school had been occupied and the strike pickets made it impossible to teach classes in a normal way, quite a few students hadn't been showing up. She would happily disappear too if she could, she confessed to Bellpuig before they went their separate ways, but she promised she would speak with Casasaies to find out what she knew about Iliescu. Anticipating the suggestion she suspected Carles Bellpuig would make about the necessity to call for a meeting of the Erasmus people, she told him she would call for one right away. If he wished, he could attend; that very morning, her secretary would let him know the day, time and place.

2

The whole November of 2008, the School of Letters of the Universitat Autònoma de Barcelona was a boiling cauldron of meetings.

Downstairs, in the occupied corridors and classrooms, the students met in permanent sessions to plan alternatives to regulated instruction, to discuss how and when to call for assemblies, what items to prioritize on the day's agenda and which would be the best strategy to continue their resistance.

Upstairs, in the departmental offices, the professors met to ponder what was going on downstairs. Some were quite happy with the situation. Not all was lost if the students had awakened from their apathy and expressed their disagreement with the system. *Gaudeamus*. About time! Some even took part in the meetings downstairs and helped design the protest programs. Others believed that this kind of awakening was not the most appropriate. Wasn't the occupying gang a minority that prevented the majority from attending classes? The majority wanted instruction and was loath to waste a whole year. A third group blamed what was happening upon a failing authority and insisted that the pickets should be expelled by force and told to go and protest at the main offices of Caixabank, the Banc de Sabadell or the women's floor of any Corte Inglés department store. Or better yet, at the *Pati dels Tarongers* of the Palace of the *Generalitat*. If those spots were too distant from their homes, the protesters could take their mattresses and sleeping bags, their butane gas stoves and food to any bank branch in the area where surely they'd be offered *cava* and *caviar canapés* ...

All of them requested to meet with the dean to give her advice, threaten her, yell at her or whatever. In response, the dean decided to call a meeting just as both Bellpuig and Casasaies had suggested. One more meeting, sure, why not?

At ten o'clock sharp on Friday, 28th November, Dolors Adrover, with professors Casasaies and Bellpuig "–I count on your support" she told them – received a small committee of students. Two girls and one boy: Laura Cremona, her friend Domenica Arrigo, also an Italian, and Marcel Bru. Homely and small, with his face the yellowish and grainy color of a lemon sorbet and his thin-rimmed round eyeglasses, Bru looked quite a lot like Leon Trotsky, a fact that Professor Bellpuig who had been a Trotskyite in his youth did not fail to notice. If the three of them had dressed differently, he in serge cloth with little bells attached, the girls in ankle-length skirts and brocade bodices, Bru would have appeared like a jester in the company of two fairy-tale princesses. Both girls were tall and pretty, especially Laura, a blonde, with the beauty of a Botticelli nymph, but one who had managed to lose twenty pounds. Both wore tight-fitting t-shirts reaching just to their belly buttons. As they sat around the conference table in the dean's office, their miniskirts revealed well-proportioned thighs which the seating arrangement of Bellpuig's classroom had obscured; he could now admire them to his heart's content. None of the students could mind his ogling. Why did they dress that way, he rationalized, if not to display such bounty of leg?

The dean's voice shook Bellpuig from his not at all metaphysical reflection. Dolors Adrover was addressing the only agenda item for that day's meeting: the measures to be taken, if any, regarding Constantinu Iliescu's disappearance. Even though she did not voice her conditional phrase out aloud, having been the dean of the School of Letters now for three years, she thought inaction the best path to follow.

"Unfortunately, early in the school year, a very high percentage of students disappear from classes, never again to set foot on the campus," she told them. "If you'd like, I could give you the exact number." She got up, went to the phone, dialed her secretary and asked for the statistics of the absenteeism that from 2000 on kept growing, year in and year out. None of the young people who had abandoned their studies had been kidnapped and none had been murdered, she stated vehemently.

"Nor have they been devoured by any ogre," Casasaies added. Besides having greeted them, she hadn't said a word and spoke now simply to reinforce the dean's opinion.

Considering the naïveté of these students, dogged as they were to think their friend had suffered some horrible fate, the reference to the children's story seemed to her most to the point.

Laura Cremona, with whom Iliescu had a romantic relationship, was quite obstinate. She insisted that Constantinu had not disappeared *motu propio* and then she paused to avoid breaking into tears.

The Latin phrase startled Carles Bellpuig, but then he recalled that the Italian educational system still taught the classical language which had been eliminated from the Catalan high schools. It sounded so strange coming from such a young mouth. "None of our teenagers would be able to utter such a phrase," he mused.

"Constantinu never failed to alert me if he couldn't make it on time," Laura continued.

Casasaies interrupted her with a question she thought relevant, even though the girl might be offended.

"How long have you two been going out together?"

"A month," she replied and suspecting the professor was questioning their relationship, she added, "but I know him well…I am sure something has happened to him." She began to sob.

Domenica Arrigo, seated next to her, stroked her hair and kissing her on the cheek told her in Italian not to cry.

Bru gave Casasaies a look of contempt as if blaming her for his friend's tears. Perhaps to placate the students, Casasaies asked Laura if she wanted a glass of water and also offered water to her companions. The three declined.

The girl's tears had caught the professors by surprise. Bellpuig, who detested seeing women cry, rose and went to the window. It was a splendid morning and the view through the glass to his left had no buildings. But the spot was condemned. The work promised during the latest Grounds Committee meeting he had to attend would soon begin there. He thought the committee's name both artificial and surrealistic. A specialist in art history and one of the most highly revered professors in the School of Letters, he was also one of the oldest members of the university. He had seen the first buildings come up in that new university, a place that was to be so different from all the others, over a terrain with grazing sheep and a soil full of black worms. What a difference from today's Leviathan of a campus! But even more different were the ideas of today in contrast with the founders' ideals. Bellpuig smiled at his thoughts, as if to apologize to himself. Perhaps, it was as much of an exaggeration to call his generation's convictions "ideals" as to call "ideas" the banal materialism of the day summarized in the extraordinarily blunt motto: "A professor who flunks his students, flunks himself."

He returned to the table when he saw that, thanks to some tissues the dean had offered, Laura had quietly wiped her nose and dried her tears. Domenica Arrigo was now speaking. She insisted that in truth Laura always said that Constantinu never failed to warn her if he was late and it made no sense that the day he had decided to move in with them to the Vila apartment, he would not show up.

After her, Cremona took over. Her fears were real. Constantinu had not picked up his cell phone for seven days now, wasn't answering his e-mail and she had no way to contact him. She did not know his address, only that it was in the Gràcia neighborhood. No one else in his or her class knew it either.

"It's strange, isn't it?" Casasaies said, trying to recall Iliescu. It was truly strange that if they dated, Cremona wouldn't know where he lived. Casasaies did not know him because he wasn't enrolled in any of her classes and could have seen him only at one of the orientation sessions, and those had a lot of people.

Instead of agreeing or dissenting, Cremona simply said that the address must have shown in his academic record which the registrar's office had refused to let them see.

Marcel Bru sided with her at once. Looking admiringly at her, he uttered words that would surely have provoked great applause in one of the anti-Bologna assemblies downstairs: "By claiming they uphold our right to privacy, they deny us access to data they insist we have no right to. Fuck! What the fuck are they depriving us for?!"

They needed the information because they were determined to find Iliescu wherever he might be. Besides, who could tell that he hadn't had a stroke and died at home without anyone knowing?

"And so, we ask," he continued, "we *demand* to be given all the information. Fuck! Stop withholding things from us!"

Considering Marcel Bru's conclusive impassioned plea, Rosa Casasaies reflected that things were always the same, that even in the minority, it was men who spoke for all. She did not think that Bru was the only one fluent in the language. Even though Laura's Catalan was quite good, it was always more effective to express oneself in one's language rather than in the one acquired in school. As for Domenica, she had opened her mouth only to corroborate what her friend had said.

★

Although the dean wasn't worried about the students considering the disappearance just another instance of absenteeism, he asked Professor Casasaies to look into the matter. She should get in touch with the family, find out where Iliescu lived in Barcelona and check whatever was necessary. If she thought it advisable, after a prudential time, she should inform the police about the disappearance. She told them that for the moment she did not think it necessary to involve the police, lest the school appear ridiculous. Not to mention the fact that doing so could damage Iliescu, bringing about disagreeable consequences in the future. Or had they already contacted the police?

"Yes," Bru answered. After his last intervention, he seemed to have anointed himself as the spokesperson.

Bru himself had gone to the police station of Sants-Montjuïc, his neighborhood, but the police paid no attention to him. He added that they told him the same thing as the dean was now telling them, as though suggesting that the dean and the police were in cahoots as the strikers claimed.

Dolors Adrover pretended not to notice the sarcastic undertone of the fake Trotsky and kept insisting she saw nothing strange in the fact that Iliescu had not been seen.

"I imagine you have checked with the hospitals," she said.

"Yes, we've done that," Bru answered. "Fuck, we're not stupid!" He locked eyes with the dean.

"Then we shouldn't worry and certainly not panic," Rosa Casasaies concluded, attempting to put an end to the staring contest.

The dean brought the meeting to an end and dismissed the students with assurances that she'd do all she possibly could to find their comrade. She again asked Casasaies to contact Iliescu's family that very morning and, as soon as she learned something, inform her at once and also the rest of the committee. She explained that if she did not offer to take care of the matter personally and delegated it to the professor, it was because she was more than busy with the school being occupied by protesters. This made it impossible for classes to take place or forced them to be taught furtively in some recondite seminar room which lent further support to the idea that Iliescu, as so many other students, had decided not to come near Bellaterra.

As soon as the students left, the dean asked her colleagues what they thought of the whole thing. She thought Laura Cremona was hysteric and had spread her hysteria to her companions and especially to Bru.

"It could be that what she cannot accept is that Iliescu has dumped her and she's created this charade out of nothing," Casasaies offered. "She can't stomach it. Her pride prevents her."

"What do you think, Carles?" The dean addressed her male colleague. "You know them."

"Yes, they're on my roster, but with the few class meetings we've had so far, I cannot tell you much. However, I have some of their papers and I seem to remember Iliescu's was one of the few notable ones; it showed his intelligence."

3

Professor Rosa Casasaies and her colleague Carles Bellpuig went to the registrar's office to have a look at Iliescu's transcript. The document listed his home address as La Palomera, a hostel in the Raval neighborhood of Barcelona. "Quite far from Gràcia," Bellpuig thought wryly. The student's permanent address was an apartment on a certain street in Bucharest. Fortunately, he had noted down his phone numbers.

Having copied the details on a "Post-it" note, Rosa Casasaies decided to go up to her office to make the phone calls in a more convenient and discreet way and then she would proceed to share her findings with the dean and Bellpuig. While Bellpuig walked to his office, at some distance from Casasaies's, to look for Iliescu's paper, she sat at her desk which was quite messy with paperwork and picked up the receiver.

She began with the hostel. They told her Iliescu was not lodging there and no one by that name had requested a room during the month of November. She had to be insistent for them to look up if the student had been there in previous months. She was put on hold for a long time and was finally told that Iliescu had spent three days in La Palomera, from 31st August to 2nd September.

She then "Googled" to see where the street in Bucharest noted in the transcript was and whether, as she suspected, the block was close to Bucharestring, the avenue where Ceausescu had erected the finest example of his megalomania – the unfinished and monstrous Palace of the People, the second largest administrative complex in the world after the Pentagon. The Romanians said that the place was still haunted by the ghosts of those who died during its construction, a work that had devastated and even razed the whole neighborhoods. Still half-empty, Casasaies had visited it as the seat of parliament. In fact, the address supplied by Iliescu was not far from the mausoleum, the *mastaba* of the dictator. Maybe Iliescu's father had been a member of the old Seguritate.

Curious to see what response she would get, she dialed the number. Luckily, she got an immediate answer. She asked in English if she'd got the home of Constantinu Iliescu. She was calling from the Universitat Autònoma de Barcelona. A woman's voice spoke to her in Romanian. Even though she had studied the language when she was young, she was not sure of understanding what she was being told and asked her if she spoke English, French, Spanish or Catalan. There was a silence. She waited a few minutes. A pleasant male voice informed her in flawless English that he would be happy to translate their conversation, and again Rosa Casasaies asked about Iliescu. Constantinu did not live there, that wasn't his home. He had lived there some time ago. The landlady, Ioana, rented out one of the two rooms in her small apartment to students because her income did not go far enough. Things were always hard in Romania. Constantinu left without any forwarding address, and she did not have one for a relative. In fact, the boy never spoke about his family; he was very reserved.

"If you see him, tell him," the man concluded, "to send Mrs. Ioana a postcard and to stop by when he returns to Bucharest."

Casasaies did not reveal the reason for her call, nor did the landlady request the interpreter to ask her. The professor did not insist on asking if the landlady knew the whereabouts of Iliescu's parents. She thought it useless.

She then called the University of Bucharest and waited a long time before she was connected to its international office. When she could finally speak to a human being, she was told the director was not in and neither was his secretary. They had left for a meeting at the Bureau and she should try again next Monday, for today was Friday. They regretted being unable to give her any reference about Constantinu Iliescu. They did not have the authority to do so. She asked for the director's e-mail address and decided to write to him, even though she thought he wouldn't look at his e-mail over the weekend. In her message, she explained that Iliescu had not showed up at the university for quite a few days and she wanted to know if he had gone back to Romania. Could he give her the student's family address? She did not elaborate about the presumed disappearance. She also thought that Iliescu had decided for personal reasons not to move to Bellaterra, that he would eventually surface, that there was no need to do anything other than calming his friends' nerves.

She then e-mailed the dean, explaining the results of her investigation, and also Laura Cremona, simply passing on the addresses in Barcelona and Bucharest, but without including the phone numbers. She could find the hostel's number on the Web; the landlady's she did not share because she did not want her pestered. After all, the landlady knew nothing about Iliescu's home and whereabouts. She found nothing strange in having shared the Bucharest address even when she knew it was not valid; it was the one on his passport; the hostel's was the address he had given the registrar when he had finalized his enrollment.

*

The first thing Professor Bellpuig did when he returned to his office was look for the picture of Iliescu in the class roster. The subject matter of Bellpuig's course for the Erasmus students was a mixed bag. Under the title "Spanish Culture," he could choose to lecture about such diverse things as Velázquez's painting and Valencian *paella*, Almodóvar and Cervantes. He had accepted teaching the course because it offered him a convenient class-meeting time and also because he was curious to know if the opinion today's European youngsters had of Spain differed from that of people his age; if kids today still thought of Spain exclusively as a country of bullfights, flamenco and castanets. He would often pause in between his lectures to seek the views of his students in this regard.

Racking his brain, he thought he remembered Iliescu intervening two or three times with comments; he appeared to be an intelligent type, more cultivated than the rest, as was the norm with students from Eastern Europe. But Bellpuig wasn't quite sure. He might be confusing his student with someone else. He had students from Poland, Hungary, Slovakia...On the other hand, he could have sworn that neither Laura nor her friend had ever opened their mouths in class, and as for Trotsky, he wasn't enrolled in his course. He had noticed the Italians because they were hot. Yet today, Laura had seemed to him an unbearably stubborn, neurotic brat. Iliescu could be avoiding her regardless of her good looks.

He opened the drawer where he kept the students' papers that he should have returned the last day he tried to meet his class. He could not teach because a picket blocked the entrance to his classroom. From the virtual campus, his teaching assistant, who had graded the exercises, told the students to pick up their papers from the professor's office, but few followed up. Of the thirty enrolled, only three students came to retrieve them.

Searching for Iliescu's paper, Bellpuig thought of the perplexed glances of those who were following his exposition on Baroque painting – the theme for the first paper he had assigned – as he compared via PowerPoint, Zurbarán's still life paintings with those of Georg Flegel's, a German painter he greatly admired, on whose work he was preparing a lecture with the title "Life, Almost Still."

"Is anyone here from Germania?" he asked.

As no one answered, he insisted:

"No? No? We'll respect their anonymity if they won't help us by sharing what they know about Flegel," he said sarcastically, since there were two students from Humboldt-Universität zu Berlin in his class.

As the two German girls pretended they hadn't even heard, he went on with questions about the paintings: "Flegel is not well known, even though he painted about a hundred still lifes of an extraordinary, realistic beauty. Observe," he told them, as he projected the painter's work onto the classroom wall, "that near the fruits, the flowers, the flasks of wine or the fishes, there always appears some nasty creature or bug. Not casually. If Flegel inserts them, it's because he wants us to know what they mean. Compare these lifes-almost-still by Flegel to those by Zurbarán. You don't have to do this now, you can look them up online or, if you prefer, in art books from the library and then drop a short essay with your conclusions into my mailbox. You will see that Spanish painting is not always more realistic than its European counterpart as is so often claimed. Regarding the notion of *vanitas*, if you go to Madrid, I highly recommend you visit the Prado. Pay attention there to the paintings by Pieter van Steenwyck."

Bellpuig went suddenly quiet. How could they possibly care about *vanitas*? They were symbols of the ephemeral, an evidence of death's siege, but none of those kids had yet felt the voracious bite of time…He cast an envious glance at them.

"Time is the main enemy of humans," he continued out loud, "but you, the young, don't know that yet and perhaps you are better off this way. By the way, *Carpe Diem* is the name of a discotheque in Barcelona nicknamed 'La Carpa.'"

Now, going over the students' exercises, he remarked that almost all his students mentioned that Zurbarán's paintings did not contain nasty elements. Only one, Iliescu, as a matter of fact, tried to explain the difference between the two painters. He wrote in a tiny, pointy and convoluted hand. Bellpuig liked his conclusion: "In a way, Flegel wants to say the same thing as the classical sentence *latet anguis in herba* – 'a snake lies in the grass.' The counterpoint between life and death does not appear in Zurbarán, even though Eros and Thanatos are bedfellows. Zurbarán does not refer to this in his still lifes or at any rate in those I have been able to see. I have read that Flegel's painting could be considered a precursor of the *vanitates*, those paintings that feature a human skull to remind us of our mortality."

Even though all that Iliescu had written could have been copied from some book, the fact that he had bothered to look it up was an indication of his interest and besides, it was well written and showed maturity.

Then he looked for Laura Cremona's essay. "I like Zurbarán better," she had written. "I think that Flegel should not paint flies or mosquitoes." This was all she said in a large English-style hand and she signed with a flourish in the shape of a cloud.

There was quite a difference between the two essays. Beauty and intelligence attracted each other. He thought of Marilyn Monroe and Arthur Miller. This wasn't the same, though. What kind of relationship must Cremona and Iliescu have had? A short relationship, to be sure: four weeks. Curiously, half the duration of his own affair with Anna Estrany; they'd been lovers for two months and he was already tired of her, his latest prey, just as Iliescu was tired of Laura. Perhaps he had decided to leave Cremona for a smarter girl and Cremona had created that brouhaha because she could not believe that he had dumped her.

4

On Friday, 28th November, the same day of the meeting called by the dean, Laura Cremona shocked everyone by appearing on *Telenotícies Vespre*, the Catalan TV3's evening news.

Spectacularly dressed and made up like a *Vogue* model – she was wearing too many clothes to be on a *Playboy* cover – she played an extraordinarily convincing role in front of the cameras as she announced the disappearance of Constantinu Iliescu, her boyfriend, with whom she was madly in love. The young man, she insisted, had gone missing between Barcelona and Bellaterra on 21st November, just one week earlier. She asserted in pained outrage that the police and the academic authorities did not even bother to recognize his disappearance. The professors, she went on, paid more attention to the occupation of the university by strike pickets than to what might have happened to Iliescu.

"How is that possible?" asked the interviewer as though he had caught Cremona's righteous indignation. "Do you mean to say they haven't responded despite you and your friends informing them about the case?"

The tearful Laura held up a poster, like the ones they had placed all over the campus, so that the cameraman – if he could stop drooling over her – could focus on Iliescu's picture. She replied that it was unfortunately so, that she had been ignored and that's why she was very thankful to TV3 for allowing her to spread the message about the disappearance of her mate. She was convinced that things found a solution only when the media intervened. She spoke softly, which highlighted her sadness, but also quite firmly.

★

Laura's appearance on *Telenotícies* stunned Rosa Casasaies who happened to see the broadcast of the interview and managed to tape all of it except for the first few seconds. On Fridays, Rosa and her husband drove to Pals on the Costa Brava where they owned a house which had no TV. This weekend, however, they stayed in Barcelona because they'd been invited to a wedding on Saturday. That's why Rosa was sitting on the sofa with her husband, surfing channels.

For the duration of the interview and even afterwards, until she finally fell asleep, Rosa kept asking herself what connections the Italian must have had to appear on TV. Rosa imagined how bothered the dean would be when she found out and how their rivals would gloat: "Now they not only have pickets occupying the school at Bellaterra, they also have to deal with missing students!" She could imagine the juicy gossip among colleagues from other universities. She imagined that the rector would call her to order. Wasn't she the person responsible for the Erasmus scholars at the School of Letters? And was it true that she did not pay any attention to them? It was clear that since last year, from the time that band of lunatics invaded the dean's office, breaking furniture and computers and wounding two security men, everyone at the School of Letters had been cursed. They'd been hexed; some sorcerer had done voodoo on them.

Fortunately, her husband soothed her: "But don't you see, all this girl wants is publicity? She is quite the actress, that much is obvious. She could even have fabricated this story of Iliescu's disappearance. What this Cremona wants is to land a job as a model or as presenter for shows, I can tell. She's the one who ought to be investigated. Call her family, ask her friends. I'd say she's a fame-whore."

Albert Vallhonrat was a psychologist specializing in child and adolescent psychology. He shared an office with a psychiatrist in the Barcelona Eixample. It was a profitable office, and even though he looked like a child–devouring ogre with hairy hands and eyebrows like brushes, he quickly earned the trust of almost everyone who visited his office. He also had a reputation for solving difficult cases. Rosa felt reassured when his examination of Cremona produced a diagnostic: "It's quite possible that in her home country she wanted to be a *velina*."

As Rosa looked at him with a puzzled air, he explained: "It's the girls in brief roles you see on game shows. If they are good, they end up as presenters. It seems that in Italy, teenage girls are obsessed with this. There are many on Berlusconi's television. For many of them, to appear on TV is more important than winning the European lottery, big pot and all."

Albert explained what his conclusion was based on and why he thought the way he did and he ended, as was usually the case in their conversations, with comparisons between the time when they wanted imagination to be in power, wanted to change the world, bring down the system, find a more just global order, and the present time, when most of the young weren't worried about armed conflicts or hunger or the rights of women in Islamic countries.

"They think the world is just fine if they're having fun. This is also what your daughter believes," he told Rosa.

He said "your" instead of "our," as he did whenever he referred to Cristina in a negative way. And also, as always, ended up stating that he wasn't blaming the young and in any case, their own generation ought to be blamed since they failed to bring about what they preached.

★

On Saturday, 29th November, at about ten o' clock in the morning, Rosa Casasaies telephoned the dean. She hadn't dared to call her the night before because she thought it was too late. She was unfamiliar with the dean's habits and thought she might not be a night person, unlike herself. Rosa just wanted to know whether the dean had seen the program and what she thought of it. Dolors Adrover told her she hadn't seen it, but knew what had taken place. An incensed Rafel Capllonc, the Defender of the Students, had called her cell at 7:30 that morning. How was it that no one had told him about Iliescu's disappearance? And how was it that the rector did not know either? Why hadn't they been informed? The dean simply answered that they had informed the office of the vice-rector for International Affairs on that very Friday afternoon by e-mail, after she had received the news from the Erasmus student adviser of her school and that she shouldn't be held responsible beyond that.

Capllonc, the Defender of the Students, was a sanguine type who from the start took everything as a matter of life and death. He also seemed to take his job quite literally and very seriously indeed. The students who went to his office with an accusation, demand or complaint, however irrelevant, absurd or foolish, emerged from the meeting satisfied and sure of Capllonc's help. It was a different matter for him to go beyond kind words and have real concern. He would take action only in extreme cases. For the rest, he came up with excuses: that university bureaucracy was slow, that his memorandum, favorable, of course, to the student had moved on to the advisory council and so on. His inaction, however, was quite effective. With the system he used, he did not have to confront professors or the administrative and service personnel – the main causes of the sorrows, travails or injustice inflicted on the poor students. But that ill-starred morning he'd been woken by a call from Catalunya Ràdio and he felt too sleepy to dodge them or mollify them with one of his cordial expressions, "oozing trotters' fat" – a phrase he recalled perhaps from his Galician mother's cooking – and was forced to admit he knew nothing of Iliescu's disappearance to the great satisfaction of the head of the weekend news section. His ignorance supported the idea that poor Laura Cremona had offered: if the university authorities were as paralyzed as they seemed, it was little wonder that the conflict with the strikers had dragged on for so long. Capllonc had cut a ridiculous figure, which he found truly unforgivable. He needed a scapegoat and had found one.

"I don't get it, Dolors," he said to the dean, furious. "I can't fathom why you didn't inform me. Am I the Defender of the Students or am I not?" He interrogated her without paying attention to what she was telling him over and over.

"It's they, the students, who had to inform you. They didn't come to me either. The campus is full of posters announcing Iliescu's disappearance. You didn't see them?" The dean did not recall that she had failed to notice them too. But Capllonc wasn't listening. He, who knew so well how to have his cake and eat it too, had had a big breakfast and come close to choking. Someone had to pay.

The dean phoned the rector as soon as Capllonc hung up, but there was no answer. It was Saturday. Perhaps the rector tried to take a break from university affairs on weekends. On the other hand, Dolors Adrover couldn't disconnect. She was obsessed by her job. She had run for the dean position, eager to better the school, improve education and the enthusiasm of professors, aid the good relationships between members of the faculty, etc. From the moment of her nomination, she had worked tirelessly day and night in the office and at home, weekdays and weekends, and yet she had failed. Her intentions, based on the principles of coeducation, laicism and student input which she had inherited from her parents, professors and from her teacher – who later became her husband – had proved completely useless. But to accept her failure implied renouncing the principles that gave meaning to her life, so she remained tied to the School of Letters at Bellaterra. When her thesis adviser, who had moved from the old university to the newly created Autònoma, asked her to join him, she did not have a moment's hesitation. Inflamed with her certainty that she would change the world of the classroom by teaching Latin, she thought it was the best thing that could have happened to her. She worked hard, engaged in research and entered the contest for a position. In the early eighties, when Robert Camós, toward the end of his career and suffering from prostate cancer, wrote to her a verse epistle – in the best Ciceronian manner and a style halfway between the *Anthologia Palatina* and the *Ars Amatoria* – proposing marriage, Dolors Adrover was not coy. Even though she considered herself an agnostic, she decided that God existed, but that heaven was on this earth. The unfortunately short years of her marriage – Camós died soon thereafter – were her happiest. After his death, she immersed herself even more in university tasks, feeling doubly obligated to do so and strove to make known the work of her late husband in the ever-shrinking circle of classicists. At first, she kept socializing with Robert's friends, all Latinists, meeting them for coffee on Thursday afternoons at the Ateneu, where they bemoaned the plight of the dead language, who could be interested in Latin now that it had disappeared from the high school curriculum and wasn't even the language of the Church? Dolors Adrover accepted the situation sadly, but she still believed that the waves of change in the country – that new-found democracy that would make them freer, cleaner, smarter and happier – had its cornerstone in education. That's why she ran for the deanship. She understood her task at the university as a mission that wasn't bound by class meeting times but stretched far and wide. However, right now, with her school occupied, she found it difficult to accept that those whose responsibility was greater than hers could leave for the weekend or simply not answer their phones as the rector was doing. Whenever a colleague, noticing her stressed condition, told her to take it easy, to take a couple of days off, she would stare at her with perplexed eyes, as though at her age, close to fifty, with the parrot nose she'd always refused to have fixed and the after-effects of her polio that, at times, forced her to limp, she had just been asked to enter the Miss World contest.

That Saturday morning, Dolors Adrover resorted to listening to music – something she did whenever she felt lonely and sad. She drew the blinds, put on a CD of Mozart's *Requiem* – the piece her husband liked most – sat down on her couch and told him, as if he were actually there, what most worried her. She exerted herself for a smooth translation because on solemn occasions, they used to communicate in Latin in remembrance of the epistle with which he had proposed to her. She said to him: "Do you know, my love? I feel like I'm sinking, problems rain on me from all directions and I've had a terrifying premonition: Laura Cremona is but an instrument to undermine the Autònoma's prestige. The disappearance of Iliescu, who by this time probably flits about fresh as a rose, unaware of the debacle provoked by his not showing up in Bellaterra, is an excuse to further stoke the fire…and I suspect there is someone pulling the strings behind this mess with the occupying students and the Erasmus scholars."

5

"The number you have dialed is not answering or out of reach," the recorded voice repeated each time Rosa Casasaies or Dolors Adrover tried to connect with Laura Cremona early the following Monday. They found it strange that there was no answer. Hadn't she assured them that she'd have her phone ready night and day in case someone called with news about her missing boyfriend? Casasaies asked herself this while waiting with the dean at the reception desk of the rectorate for a meeting with the head of the university. Eventually, Dolors Adrover had managed to contact the rector late Sunday afternoon and he requested they meet to watch the tape of the interview and, along with the vice-rector for International Affairs, discuss the advisability of issuing a statement to the press in conjunction with the Defender of Students. Luckily for the dean, who had no desire to meet the rector, Capllonc was unable to attend the meeting because he'd been summoned quite some time ago to a meeting of the Museu d'Art Contemporani de Barcelona (MACBA) on the board of which he sat and would be late getting to the university.

The rector's administrative assistant, a woman who sat at her desk in the spacious and well-furnished office suite, volunteered her opinion. She had seen the interview and, as many of the Autònoma's personnel, was curious. "It could well be that Friday's program allowed the girl to find Iliescu. Didn't she say that things get solved only when the media intervene? I think she's right," she concluded.

Neither she nor the receptionist believed, as the two Letters professors now realized that the whole thing was a kind of soap opera devised by the Erasmus students. They thought it was difficult to pull the wool over the eyes of the best news program of Catalan television; they must have done some research before interviewing the girl.

After she had listened to the same taped message from Laura's cell at least thirty times, Casasaies decided to call Marcel Bru. He told them Domenica had called him on Saturday, uneasy because Laura had not returned home and he gave the professors her number. Domenica too answered right away. She happened to be at the school, on her way to the adviser's office. She was going there to ask for help. She was very worried because since Friday night, she'd had no news from Laura. When Laura left the television studios at 10:15 p.m. that night, she had sent Domenica a text telling her she was going to have a beer with a friend and she wouldn't be too late, but she had not returned.

★

Later that morning, Rosa Casasaies took an edgy and scared Domenica Arrigo to Cerdanyola; the Universitat Autònoma was assigned to the police station there. On the way, the young woman explained tearfully that she had the premonition she would never again see her friend, vanished like Iliescu, between Barcelona and Bellaterra. Casasaies's insistence that she was sure Cremona was hale and hearty and would make her appearance soon was of no use. Useless also were her attempts to calm Domenica with optimistic conjectures: Iliescu might have seen the interview and they had gotten together and were still celebrating or Laura had spent the weekend at the place of the friend she was going to have a beer with where she could not charge her cell. Who was that friend? Did Domenica have any idea?

"No."

Once, she said sobbing, Laura had mentioned some friends from Milan who lived in Barcelona, but she did not believe her friend had gone to them. Besides, if that's what she'd intended, why announce she would be home soon?

"Do you know the names of those friends? Where they live?"

"No. She spoke about one Giovanni, an Erasmus scholar at the Universitat Pompeu Fabra..." She couldn't recall anything else.

★

Manuela Vázquez, the sub-inspector of the investigative unit, who received Rosa Casasaies and Domenica Arrigo after the Italian had filed the missing persons report at the Cerdanyola police station, asked her to make an effort and recall all she could about her friend. It was very important. The more data they had, the easier it would be to arrive at some conclusion.

The sub-inspector was not a pessimist or at least, she didn't seem so, especially after watching the DVD with the *Telenotícies* interview that, along with a poster with Iliescu's photograph, Casasaies had brought along. Manuela Vázquez became aware at once of Cremona's craving for attention. Perhaps making her friends worried when she didn't show up was part of the same strategy. She'd seen plenty of cases like that. They'd all been motivated by a desire for a leading role.

Manuela was a rather short and vivacious woman, very affable, but also blunt. In college, she had majored in psychology and specialized in gender violence. As a member of the national police, before she joined the autonomous Mossos d'Esquadra, she had been assigned to investigate charges of abuse at the Ciutat Vella station in Barcelona. Whether or not the complaints she received were real or fake, she almost always got it right at first glance. She had no doubt that Domenica spoke the truth, but the disappearance of the two students from the campus may have been deliberate, a result of seeking attention. Perhaps the matter was simply that and not two kidnappings or worse, as Domenica supposed. She tried to calm Domenica.

"I understand you are worried, but I want you to know that most disappearance cases get resolved positively. I can assure you," she insisted. "Only one-tenth of 1% of the reported cases are considered real risk, and neither of your friends falls in this category. They are both over twenty-one and mentally balanced; they are not children or seniors with dementia. But let me check if there is news about Iliescu."

The sub-inspector left the room and came back after a couple of minutes.

"As soon as the guys from the Sants station know something, they'll let me know. They've been in touch with the police in Romania. The Sants guys suspect Iliescu has left Barcelona. He has disappeared," she made the gesture for quotation marks, "by his own volition."

"That's what I think too," Rosa Casasaies said. "But I do not think he's gone back to his country. Or if he has, he hasn't gone to the University of Bucharest. At the international office there, they believe he is here or at least that's what they told me in reply to the e-mail I sent them on Friday."

"If so many husbands tell their wives 'I'm going to buy a pack of cigarettes' and never come back, what won't unmarried types do?" The sub-inspector wondered in a relaxed tone and with a rather soft, reassuring voice to try and calm Domenica.

Manuela Vázquez had seen only the picture of Iliescu on the flyer she had on her desk and so she didn't dare reach any conclusions. From the picture, he seemed to be quite a handsome young man with a shy and woeful air, quite the opposite of Laura's. The taped images of Laura's interview were most eloquent. Everything – her posture, the way she moved, how she tossed her hair off her face or crossed her legs and the outfit she wore – indicated that she wanted to attract, to awaken interest, to be looked at…But the policewoman told this only to Casasaies when Domenica had left them to go to the bathroom, perhaps because a certain complicity had developed between the two older women. They had some things in common: they were rather plump, wore eyeglasses and were probably the same age. They were alike even in the way they dressed: similar jackets, luckily not the same color, made in China, imported by Inditex and bought at Zara. Besides, the fact that Vázquez was a college graduate reassured Casasaies who tended to think that people who had been to university were less dumb than the rest. Despite her distrust of the police, a remnant of her anti-Franco progressive days, the professor had to admit that things had changed a lot, at least in appearance, at the *mossos* police stations. And she was pleased to see that despite her skepticism regarding the disappearance of the Erasmus scholars, the sub-inspector set to work and assured them that the first thing she'd do would be to phone the television station. It could be that Laura Cremona did not go there alone, in which case they should have the name and address of the person or persons who had gone along. She would also contact other friends. Domenica wrote down some names for her with the corresponding cell phone numbers. Vázquez would call them one after the other or would have agents in her team do so. But there was a call she was not eager to make, at least not right away, because she still believed that nothing had happened to Laura and she did not want to alarm her parents. She still felt the terrible pain from the time barely two years ago when a stranger's voice woke her early one morning to tell her that her daughter Sònia had been seriously injured in an accident and was in the hospital. She had felt as though her belly had been pierced by a sharp piece of glass. Vázquez asked Professor Casasaies to call Laura Cremona's parents first, so they would find some comfort in a familiar voice and be better prepared for a call from a stranger like her.

6

The rector delegated Rosa Casasaies and Antoni Capllonc, the Defender of the Students, to welcome the parents of Laura Cremona at the Barcelona airport. They had announced they would arrive on 2nd December at three o' clock in the afternoon on an Alitalia flight.

Professor Casasaies did not mind holding a placard with the name of the Universitat Autònoma over "MR. & MRS." CREMONA so that they could find them right away as they stepped out into the arrivals hall of the terminal. Antoni Capllonc, however, thought that the holding of a placard was undignified for university professors, even though he really wasn't one – he'd been hired from the publishing world where he had gained some prestige –and suggested to Casasaies to have the rector's chauffeur take care of that rather inelegant mission and offered to go find him. But as Casasaies didn't feel bad about holding the placard – she had carried or helped carry much larger ones at demonstrations in her youth – and realizing that Capllonc felt uncomfortable standing by her side as if he were the chauffeur and she a kind of subcontracted tour guide waiting for the distinguished members of some conference, she suggested to him to go have a cup of coffee and leave her with the placard.

As soon as Rosa was left alone with her placard, two very thin, tall and elegant ladies approached her. They were dressed in Armani and carried authentic Vuitton luggage (unlike Rosa's, a fake which she'd purchased in New York's Chinatown) and the professor thought they would ask for some trivial information: where the VIP parking garage was or the information booth or the rent-a-car counters. This sort of thing happened a lot to her. "This happens to you because you look like a wise owl," her husband had teased her whenever she complained that she was always the one people came to with the most outlandish and diverse requests for information. But this time she was wrong.

"I'm Clara Cremona," said the woman who looked younger and stretched out a soft-skinned hand for a powerful handshake. With a pleasant and also sad smile she added: "Thank you for coming to pick us up. Let me introduce my partner, Margaret Hogarth."

"*Piacere, professorina. Grazie tante,*" Hogarth said. "Any recent news about Laureta?" she asked in Italian and excused herself for speaking neither Catalan nor Spanish, even though, she said, she understood Spanish.

Clara Cremona by contrast, spoke fluent Spanish but with a strong Italian accent. The tone of her voice was milder and sweeter than Margaret's. The strongest features of her angular face were her eyes of a strange color, halfway between emerald and violet. Her daughter looked a lot like her, but unfortunately had not inherited her eyes.

As for Signora Cremona's companion, it was enough to see how passers-by looked at her. She was easy on the eyes, she drew admiration because she was so attractive, which a certain ambiguous air underscored. Casasaies, dressed in blue jeans and an unbranded jacket, felt insignificant next to the two of them. It was as though their mere presence made her smaller; she thought herself even shorter, chubbier, hippier. The unaffected elegance of those women, unexpected as it was, jarred her.

After the pleasantries and having assured them that Laura would sure resurface, she told them she'd come with the Defender of Students who had gone for a cup of coffee and if they weren't expecting anybody else, they could be on their way as soon as he came back. Unsure whether her reference to expecting someone else had been understood, she asked directly: "Laura's father is not coming?" In case Signora Cremona was divorced, Rosa did not say "your husband," supposing a separation was the case if she came with a friend.

"Laura has no father. We…"

Antoni Capllonc's arrival with his flourishes and bows before such glamorous ladies cut short Clara's explanation. A few minutes later, as they walked to the parking area, Signora Cremona continued with extraordinary ease and explained that her daughter did not have conventional parents.

Signora Cremona wanted to make it clear right away in order to prevent confusion and, so as not to be asked about the biological father, told them that Laura was the fruit of artificial insemination. They had married in Amsterdam where Margaret, even though she was English, had lived most of her life, and they thought of themselves indistinctly as Laura's mother and father.

Five minutes before such a revelation, it would not have crossed the minds of either Rosa Casasaies or Antoni Capllonc that the couple they were awaiting was not made of a man and a woman, but of two women. Rosa supposed that however progressive Capllonc seemed, he was at the moment wondering whether either of the women would have changed their sexual orientation if they had met a man as attractive as he. Professor Casasaies worried lest someone at the university would make a *faux pas*. She herself had already made one by inquiring about Laura's father.

Laura Cremona's mothers got to the official car which was waiting to take them to Bellaterra to meet the rector. The vice-rector for International Affairs had laid down the protocol. "Given the present circumstances, it has to be more than a bouquet of flowers. It is important that from the start, the parents feel welcome and realize that we are doing everything possible to find their daughter." After a few introductions to academic authorities, the rector himself would take them to meet the Cerdanyola Chief of Police, Inspector Martínez González, under whose command sub-inspector Manuela Vázquez served. Both of them thought it was essential to meet the parents of the girl and learn about her family life. They had seen nothing wrong in meeting them at an office of the administrative building, a more neutral venue and less loaded with negative connotations than the police station. In that room decorated with prints by Tàpies and a couple of politically themed paintings by Guinovart, its large windows overlooking the campus, the two police officers, along with the vice-rector for International Affairs – who had volunteered to serve as interpreter – sat at a round table, preparing for the meeting they would have with the family of the missing girl.

To avoid confusion or someone starting on the wrong foot, Professor Casasaies used her cell phone to alert, first the rector's secretary and then the sub-inspector, about the sexual preference of Signora Cremona and the presence of her partner. She took care of this as soon as she got out of the car, walking away from the Italians, not because she thought the rector or the police had anything against lesbians or could feel uncomfortable in their presence, but to prevent them from involuntarily making the women feel ill at ease or creating an embarrassing misunderstanding.

Nothing of this sort came about; just some gender-pronoun hesitation on the part of the inspector, whom those spectacular ladies made quite nervous. Instead of waiting for the questions he had for them, they began by interrogating him in an attempt to find out if it was true that no effort had been spared in the search for Laura and to what point they had hopes of finding her soon. Did they have any leads? What had they done from the moment Domenica had reported the disappearance? How seriously were they taking this case?

It was Manuela Vázquez who explained what she and her team had carried out during the past twenty-nine hours since taking the case. Besides Dominica, they had spoken with the Erasmus students closest to Laura and with some of her professors and had been in touch with the staff of the television program that had interviewed the girl. She insisted kindly but firmly that they could be assured that her team had taken the case seriously.

The inspector thought it was time for him and Manuela to play their roles and ask the questions. As though he had forgotten that the interpreter, seeing he was not needed, had left, he spewed out at once the questions he had jotted down for translation, reformulating them one by one after each response: What can you tell us about Laura that could give us a clue? Did she ever mention Constantinu Iliescu to you? Has she ever left home without announcing it? What is your relationship with Laura? Do you get along? Does she like Barcelona? Do you know her friends?

Because she spoke Spanish, Clara Cremona answered all of them. They had never had serious problems with Laura other than some squabbles about the time to come home at night when she began to date and some trivial arguments. Both she and Margaret thought her skirts were too short to go out on the town in. Margaret had scolded her a couple of times: "As if you weren't a born and bred Milanese, but a vulgar tourist!" But at the same time, she felt proud to have such a beautiful daughter. Clara now addressed her companion in English: "Do you remember, *cara*?"

Margaret nodded and sweetly caressed for a second the hand Clara had laid on the table. After a pause, Signora Cremona, as though regretting the boasting about her family, added that of course a daughter seemed gorgeous to any parent. She did not dwell on the fact that in this case, Laura's beauty was undeniable.

She did not say – probably, because at that time a wisely selective memory prevented her – that the relationship with her daughter was a precarious one, that once she was dating, she never paid any attention to them and let the boys she dated influence her. She had not told them about Constantinu because she rarely spoke about her sudden infatuations, short-lived, but experienced with great intensity like everything else in her life. Yet it was one thing to keep them in the dark and another for her to leave home without their knowledge. To go where? And why? She had already left home to study abroad she was so excited about. And as to the friends she could have in

Barcelona, they didn't know a thing. She had only mentioned her roommate, Domenica Arrigo.

Margaret asked if they could smoke. Neither the inspector nor the sub-inspector minded; while Vázquez left the room to find an ashtray – there was a smoke-free campus policy – Ms. Hogarth took a pack of 'More,' those long menthol cigarettes, from her bag. She waited for the sub-inspector's return to offer one first to her and then to the Chief of Police. Both declined. Then she put two cigarettes in her mouth and lit them, handing one to her partner.

"Smoke suits them," Vázquez thought, remembering the gangster movies she liked so much and in which the smoke from a cigarette was an extraordinary ingredient: it created mystery, it softened the evil harshness in the assassins' features and lent a few clouds of glory to the auras of honest detectives and incorruptible cops.

"What kind of boys did Laura go out with when she lived with you?" Manuela asked, abandoning her musings about tobacco smoke and noticing the compulsive pleasure with which the women smoked.

"Laura likes weird guys," said Signora Cremona. "Since she began to date, perhaps too young, at least in my opinion…Even today, we parents are possessive about our *bambini*." She smiled sadly. "She keeps looking for types that are set apart from most people, rather freakish. For a few months, she went out with a contortionist and she also fell in love with a black guy, a Nigerian, like those men who peddle counterfeit bags and sunglasses on the streets."

Manuela Vázquez was taking notes in a notebook she had started a day ago when she had interviewed Domenica Arrigo. On the first page she had written: "Autònoma Disappearances." Taking advantage of a pause from Signora Cremona, she said:

"From what I've been able to gather, Iliescu was also strange, if I may use this word, or at least, mysterious. Laura might have been attracted to him because of this, even though he was, he *is*," she corrected herself, "attractive." From a folder she took out a photograph of the boy and showed it to the mothers. "As

I understand, he was reserved, *is* reserved," she corrected herself again. "His friends say he was a man of few words, they didn't know where he lived, not even Laura knew it. We suspect he was short of money and might have been living out of the little van from Romania he came in as my colleagues from the Sants police station have informed me. That's why I haven't ruled out that at this very moment, the two of them might be taking a trip in the van and will return any moment."

"I should wish nothing better," Signora Cremona said softly on the verge of tears. "The only thing I want in this world is to see her again."

The inspector considered that he could grant her wish virtually and proposed they watch the previous Friday's TV interview. He had a different copy from the one taped by Professor Casasaies; his was one procured directly from the television station by Vázquez who had gone to the TV3 studios on Monday to find out how the girl had managed to bag a TV interview.

The people at the studio couldn't tell her if their department head had made the decision because he thought Laura Cremona's presence would add human interest to the news of Iliescu's disappearance – as he had put it to them at their meeting on Thursday – or whether she also had some influence at the station or some higher-up had recommended her. What they were sure about was the girl's insistence because she had called several times.

It was the head of the news bureau whom the sub-inspector finally found in Istanbul – where she was covering one of the many debates about whether Turkey would or would not join the European Union – who told her that Laura Cremona had contacted her secretary and that she gave the green light because she thought the news was of interest and not because anyone had pushed for the girl. She uttered this last phrase in an annoyed and blunt tone as if she wanted to make quite clear that what counted in her program was the newsworthiness of the information and that she did not oblige anyone who made unfair demands.

Manuela Vázquez had also found out that Laura Cremona had gone to the TV studios alone because next to hers, the log did not show any other name. But someone could have gone to pick her up. The taxi service TV3 worked with had no record of a cab being dispatched for the girl and she did not have a car. No one left the TV studios on foot, much less at night. The industrial complex where the studios stood was on a highway where pedestrians were not allowed. If Laura had meant to meet a friend, the logical thing would have been to meet that person right there. There were security cameras outside the studios. Manuela Vázquez asked to be sent the Friday tapes to see if someone had given her a ride and if that person was Iliescu.

7

Rosa Casasaies did not dare discuss Laura Cremona's family until she was back at her home for fear her colleagues would think of her as a reactionary fuddy-duddy incapable of respecting all sexual orientations. But when talking to her husband, she shared her frank surprise at the arrival of the two-women couple. She had to admit she still had some prejudices even though she hadn't thought so in the recent past. She recalled, with a bad taste in her mouth, the night she had been surprised by her prejudiced thinking. She had been returning from a conference in New York on a flight stuffed with ultra-orthodox Jews with their *kippahs* and phylacteries, reeking of sweat and reused oil. She had caught herself feeling extraordinarily repulsed and had thought if she had a way to eliminate them, she would not hesitate to do so. A reciprocated repugnance, she was sure. They not only prevented her from getting any sleep as they spent the night chanting, reading the Torah out loud or praying in groups – despite her request for silence time and again – they also looked at her as one looks at an insignificant worm before squishing it under one's shoe.

When she exited from the sardine can the airplane had become, she realized at once that what she had wished for was abominable. She could not comprehend how she had arrived at such levels of contempt for other people, however annoying or plain wrong she thought them; she who preached tolerance and acceptance of others, yes, yes, that was the word – *preached*. She was a member of *SOS Racisme*, contributed to all sorts of organizations and NGOs that fought for the rights of immigrants and, of course, loathed the Nazis.

Surely all those who had met Signore Cremona-Hogarth showed the tolerance she preached, making no remark other than about the elegance and beauty of the ladies or their concern and sadness. However, the Chief of Police did reveal his prejudice.

On the ride back from Bellaterra to the Cerdanyola station, Martínez González advanced the theory that Laura's family situation was the cause for both her preference for weird types and her need to call attention to herself. He thought it was quite nefarious that the girl had a father and a mother of the same sex or two mothers and blamed them indirectly for the girl's disappearance.

Because in his profession, the inspector was given to finding a cause for any action, he felt satisfied to have found the justification for Laura's behavior. On the other hand, for Manuela Vázquez the absence of a father, a father who shaved each morning, a father with a mustache or a beard, was not sufficient explanation to justify the fact that Laura Cremona feigned a disappearance just to be noticed or to get back at her family.

Martínez González was an impulsive man. As he stepped out of the car, a journalist from Ràdio Cerdanyola approached him to ask if there was any news, and he said yes, that he'd spoken with the moth...– but could not complete the word because Manuela Vázquez pretended to have a fainting spell and grabbed the inspector's arm so as not to fall while at the same time, with a seemingly involuntary movement, upset the microphone the journalist held. She knew that Martínez González, who had always proved to be a considerate person, would assist her before answering the journalist's questions. As the inspector helped her into the police station, he pondered whether to call for an ambulance or take her to the hospital himself, even though Vázquez insisted it was nothing, just a fainting fit-like she often had. Her ploy gave her time to warn him not to say anything about Laura's parents being mothers or father–mother. If the press got a whiff of that, the poor ladies would not have a moment's rest. They both knew that journalists considered deviations from the norm an attractive bonus to any news story.

When the inspector returned to the journalist after reassuring himself that the sub-inspector was fine, he simply said that the family of the missing girl had arrived in Barcelona and that the investigation was on the right path, but that discretion was absolutely necessary. That was all. No more questions.

Back in her office, Manuela Vázquez drank sugar water despite her strict sucrose-free diet. She wanted to lend a touch of truth to the situation and continue their discussion when Martínez González returned.

Her office, like the whole building, was new and functional, done mostly in grays and with a large window through which she could admire two rows of trees, now with fall foliage that the mild weather had not shorn from the branches – a pleasant surprise for those last days in November. She felt at home here. Her room was so different from the small, stifling office she had at the sordid Ciutat Vella station before moving to Cerdanyola. Besides, there she had to share space with three colleagues, even though the office held only two metal desks of a murky and dismal gray and a couple of chairs upholstered in vinyl with cracked seats and backs. To lighten the atmosphere and add some color to her room, she would occasionally buy herself pink and white orchids. Having become used to the cheery company of the flowers, she had also bought orchids when she arrived in Cerdanyola, but here she didn't need them as much.

"Both the radio guys and those from Cerdanyola television, who arrived a bit later," the inspector said as he entered Manuela Vázquez's office, "have saved us the trouble of issuing a press release. "No need to do it now. The more I think about it, the more I am convinced that if Laura finds out the women are here," and he inflected the word "women" with an ironic tone, "and finds out that they are worried, she will come out of her hideout by herself or with Iliescu. Don't you think so? She would have to be quite the little bitch to remain hidden once she knows what they are going through. I imagine she's got cash. We'll have to check the charges to her credit cards."

"I've taken note and am going to ask for a warrant from the judge as well as permission to enter her home if she does not show up this very day. But if, as everything seems to point out, she's got money, she could be hiding in any hostel or hotel, one of those places that do not insist on identification on checking in, because that way they don't have to declare earnings to the taxman. She may not learn of the mess she's made until she shows up again."

"I am dead sure," Martínez González continued. "She will emerge soon enough; it's all a plan she's concocted with Iliescu to punish her mothers or female fathers or whatever they are called."

With a smile, he insisted that as he had concluded from the conversation with the women – now he called them "the women" – did not get along with the daughter and the girl had never forgiven them for making her a part of a family that wasn't "normal."

Only when Manuela pointed out that in "normal" families the relationships between parents and children could be just as complicated, full of tension and all kinds of surprises, often based on misunderstandings such as the conviction that we know those we love which is not true or at least, not in most cases, only then did the inspector agree with her and recognize that he had problems getting along with his youngest son, Marc despite having a conventional family, a good, normal and average family. He didn't add, however, that, since he'd kicked his son out of his house because he was lazy, his relationship with Marc was now nonexistent, and he feared that his child would be arrested any day and brought to him in handcuffs. He knew Marc hung out with rough crowds and was probably dealing with drugs.

"Inspector, you can't deny that Laura Cremona is much luckier with her family than Iliescu was with his," said the sub-inspector. "That he's managed to make it to university is some kind of miracle. I don't know if you've had a chance to read the translation of the report that the General Bureau of the Police of Romania sent to the Sants police station. Martorell faxed it to me this morning and I have handed it to your secretary."

"I have not. What does the report say?"

"That he is an orphan or rather, that his parents abandoned him by a dumpster when he was just a few months old and he ended up in a state-run orphanage and later was moved to a middle-way house supported by funds from a Catholic charity. The guys in Sants added to the report details they got from the police in Bucharest. It looks like the middle-house director thought Iliescu much smarter than most orphans and looked after him. Given that his IQ far surpassed the average for children his age, the director strove to put him under the wing of an international organization that, after Ceacescu's fall, had opened centers in Romania to help in the education of underprivileged youths. Those people thought he ought to study beyond learning a trade. The report says Iliescu did both. He got a license as an electrician and plumber and at the same time won a scholarship to Bucharest University. His baccalaureate transcript is among those at the top of his class. He made a living working jobs at people's houses and managed to save enough to purchase his little van, the one he drove all the way to Barcelona and which now, like him, has vanished."

"Our young people ought to learn something from all that hardship," the inspector said, once again thinking of his son.

"Do you know what I think?" said Manuela. "In the relationship between Iliescu and Cremona, there is, on her part, something of the maternal instinct. This is a biological imperative that in some women, not in all, is quite strong. And who can tell if it isn't the orphaned inner child of Constantinu's that most attracted Laura?"

She got up and opened a file cabinet, extracted the flyer with Constantinu's photograph and handed it to her boss. "Look, you'll notice in his eyes a kind of ancient helplessness, the mark of a life of upsets, don't you think? I've seen the like in the faces of other immigrants."

But she stopped there, knowing that she and her superior did not see eye to eye on immigration and the problems it brought about.

The inspector returned the flyer to Manuela, and she again peered at the picture to see if she could glean anything from Iliescu's features that might help her figure out whether he had disappeared on purpose to avoid Laura, whether he felt trapped or if the lack of affection in his life prevented him from accepting or offering love. From what Domenica Arrigo had told her, it was Laura who had approached the Romanian and pursued him until she managed to capture his interest. She was used to that sort of behavior and it mattered little who the chosen one was. It could be anyone, a professor, a student or a bus driver like that young man who drove a bus on the Barcelona-Cadaqués line and whom Laura did not know from Adam, but when they arrived at the last stop, Laura suggested he give her a tour of the town and accompany her to a disco. He agreed, enthralled and euphoric. They went out for drinks, they danced and ended the night making love on the beach. But when he asked for her phone number and said he'd like to see her again, she refused. She told him, "What are you thinking? That I'm an idiot? This thing tonight is of no importance. It means nothing to me." But things were otherwise with Iliescu; she had fallen in love and did not give up until he agreed to move in with her.

8

On Wednesday, 3rd December, all the newspapers carried the news of Laura Cremona's disappearance. The radio and television stations in Catalonia also broadcast it. TV3 reran segments of the Friday, 28th November interview and gave the disappearance twice the airtime than the other channels. The fact that the student had vanished after leaving the TV3 studios in Sant Joan Despí, where she had gone to talk about another disappearance, made everyone from the director to the youngest of the interns feel more or less directly involved in the case.

There was one station, known for its antagonistic approach to Catalanism and the ultraconservative bent of its owners that blasted in Spanish: "A university occupied by rioters, with a campus where unlawful and possibly murderous types roam freely, all facts that clearly show to what point the academic authorities have lost control." The other media outlets did not dare identify the disappearance with a crime, nor did they attribute the presumed lack of campus safety to the university's governing team. Whether they had heeded the communication sent by the rector in which he requested they refrain from creating unnecessary alarm among the 40,000 students and their families or because they considered, as the police had done from the start, that both cases would soon be resolved, stations and newspapers served the news with very little morbidity.

The "Students in Love Vanish" case, as one of papers distributed for free at metro stations called it, had jumped to the Web and a number of blogs mentioned it. There were echoes in Italy also. Some related the disappearance of the couple to the November 2007 murder in Perugia just a year ago, of an English Erasmus scholar, Meredith Kercher, which involved her roommates who were also foreign students. It was supposed that the police must have already questioned those who lived with Laura Cremona and her inner circle of friends. It was a proven fact that in most homicides, the persons closest to the victim were responsible.

Domenica Arrigo's mother who read about the events online was greatly upset and unaware of the huge mistake she was making by posting a message in a chat room, stating that her daughter was innocent and should not be questioned regarding the death of her friend. Signora Arrigo's participation in the chat room had the opposite effect of the one she sought. From that moment on, a number of bloggers, mostly Italian, who had been given wings on learning the name of Laura Cremona's friend, considered Dominca guilty. They had been further prodded by what had happened with Meredith who had been killed by a knife wound to her neck inflicted by her North American roommate Amanda Knox.

Laura Cremona's family resorted to the Internet listings of disappeared persons and added a photograph of the girl and her personal data. In agreement with the police, those of Iliescu were also included. The Italian Consul, Dante Braccalente, who had invited the mothers to his house and had declared himself at their disposal, had advised them to publish the information. The consul considered that given the times, the Web reached where neither newspapers nor television did, especially among the young and the widespread postings of the images of Laura and Iliescu on the Web, whether the students had disappeared together and voluntarily or they had been captured by a band seeking ransom, even though no one had approached Iliescu's friends or Laura's family for money, might help in making an identification.

The consul thought that nothing extreme had happened to the couple, that they would emerge once the wave of passion would allow them to leave the secret lair of their idyll and so, he insisted to the Signore Cremona-Hogarth, they should not worry unnecessarily. He was trying to be as kind as he could.

Laura's biological mother was a wealthy and well-connected jewelry designer. Her partner, the adoptive mother, had served on the European Parliament in Brussels and moved with great ease among the political and intellectual circles of the European Left. For a young person with humble origins, but great ambition as was the consul, the friendship with these two could be an advantage and thus he would help them as much as he could. A *bon vivant* with highly developed taste buds, Braccalente was deeply sorry that their present stressful condition prevented the ladies from experiencing Catalan cuisine as it deserved to be enjoyed. He thought it was first-class. He insisted on taking them to Restaurant Hispania, one of the best in Catalonia in his opinion. He thought that if they tasted some of the dishes prepared by the owner-chefs Paquita and Lolita, friends of his and of most distinguished gourmets, they would forget anything that had to do with the disappearance of their daughter during the meal. But most of the dishes gave them just a short respite from their anxiety. Only when they ate the lobster stew, a specialty of the house, did they seem a bit more relaxed.

The consul's hypothesis that pleasing sensations sent to the brain by the taste buds are capable of erasing the bitterest of sorrows worked with his guests for a couple of minutes, no more. This fact, however, did not invalidate his hypothesis; he considered the ladies the exception that proves the rule. What was happening, he thought, was that the female brain was not stimulated in the same way as the male's by the pleasures of the palate. In the case of men, he had no doubt of the beneficial influence of gastronomy. He had tested it often with friends who had lost their money, were widowed or abandoned by their spouses.

Signore Cremona-Hogarth did not finish their servings, even though they protested that they tasted great, and returned to their obsession. That morning, they had been in the apartment their daughter had shared with Domenica. They had seen her clothes hanging in the closet, her books perfectly organized on shelves in her room. On her desk, a file of notes lay open. Her passport and two credit cards were in the drawer.

"If she had wanted to flee," Clara remarked, "she would have taken all that with her. Laura did not lack foresight; even if she had cash with her, her cards are tied to my account and I know she withdrew some money on Friday morning."

"How much?" The consul asked as he cast a sad glance at their leftovers which he would have eaten with delight if he had felt more at ease with his guests.

"Six hundred euros," said Clara. "Domenica told us she had spoken about meeting a private detective who could help find Iliescu and for this she might need cash. Friday afternoon she went to Barcelona. Until she appeared on the program, none of her friends saw her. We don't know what she did."

Clara went quiet. Then, almost in tears, she picked up the bag she had hung on the back of her chair and without caring about what her host or the other diners might think, she took out a tattered brown teddy bear and hugged it. Margaret stroked her hair and addressed Braccalente: "It's our daughter's favorite teddy bear...We found it on her bed. Clara wanted us to take it. Since she was a child, Laura took it wherever she went." Then, looking at her partner who was quietly weeping, she said to her: "Come now, *cara*, let's get some air." Holding her arm she led her to the garden.

9

On Thursday, 4th December, the news of Constantinu Iliescu's and Laura Cremona's disappearances spread beyond the national sphere. If the university authorities had been able, they would have avoided that mess. It was most damaging to the UAB public image. The university needed to increase the enrollment year after year, given the budget deficit it carried. The steep competition with other Catalan universities made things worse, and the investments in a series of publicity campaigns emphasizing the true level of excellence of its schools and colleges had little impact on the locals, obliging the university to rely on students from other parts of Europe. The majority of Erasmus scholars chose the Autònoma. But now, after what had happened, no one knew whether that would remain the case. The revelation that Iliescu and Cremona had vanished was a cause for alarm more for the other Erasmus students and their families than for the locals. Some who had registered for the School of Letters went so far as to decide – given that the school still did not offer classes – to take a break and go back to their countries. They had been affected not so much by the disappearance of Iliescu, whom most foreign students had not met, but by that of Cremona, an extroverted, beautiful and quite popular young woman. Many contacted Domenica Arrigo and Marcel Bru and offered to make handbills and post them throughout the university, next to those for Iliescu, despite the fact that in Laura's case, a homemade dissemination was not needed.

The students occupying the school discussed Cremona's case in their afternoon assembly. They spoke of the probability that the forces of oppression – meaning police and teachers – would hold them responsible for the disappearances. They stated that if this were to be the case, they would take irreversible measures. They were tired of being unjustly painted as instigators of all the problems the bourgeois capitalists were unable to solve.

At 4 o'clock in the afternoon, at the same time as Miquel Oliver, one of the assembly's leaders, was referring to the matter in a classroom of the School of Letters, Clara Cremona was still crying as she hugged her daughter's teddy bear in a corner of the Restaurant Hispània in Arenys de Mar. Since they had left the apartment Laura shared with her friend, both Clara and Margaret had given up on the hope that Laura disappeared of her own volition. But since they both refused to accept the worst, they made an effort to think of other possibilities that might lead, at least, to a happy ending, an ending that would let them find their daughter.

"Could it have been Giacomo? Could Giacomo have taken her away?" Margaret suddenly asked Clara, seconds before Dante Braccalente joined them along with the restaurant owners who wanted to say goodbye and ask if they had liked the food.

Clara waited to be in the consul's car before she answered that she didn't think it possible for Giacomo to have kidnapped Laura.

"Who is this Giacomo?" The consul asked them. He was interested in that possibility which neither of them had mentioned to him, despite the long hours they had spent going over the same obsession.

"Laura's father," Clara replied. She was no longer crying. "My ex-husband. He renounced his paternity many years ago and that's why I always say my *bambina* is the product of artificial insemination. I don't think he even knows Laura is here."

"But remember that he is from here," Margaret said, very serious. "And perhaps he needs money. He sold the renunciation of his paternity rights for quite a sum and that was not enough for him. It wouldn't be the first time he's tried to blackmail us."

"Have you mentioned this possibility to the police?" the consul asked.

The women shook their heads and Clara added, but only to her partner, as if she had forgotten the consul was there: "If he had kidnapped Laura, he would have already gotten in touch with us to ask for money. Besides, he hasn't seen her for many years. Laura is a stranger to him. No, I do not think this possibility is worth even considering…And don't tell me again that you did not want her to come to Barcelona or that I didn't see any danger in the fact that her father had been born here. We don't even know if he lives here now. And besides, how could he have known that Laura is a student here when he's never had any contact with her?"

Margaret did not answer any of those questions. She simply said in a low voice, as if speaking to herself: "I have a terrible premonition, *cara*." And she got her cell phone from her bag and offered it to Clara: "Please give Bianca a call and ask her if there is a message for you or a letter or an e-mail to the office. He doesn't have your cell phone number, right?"

Clara Cremona did not pick up the phone her partner offered her, but she got hers out and dialed her secretary. When she hung up after a brief conversation, she said there was no message that could involve Laura's father, but before she put the phone away, she heard the beep of an incoming message. It was from the police station at Cerdanyola. The sub-inspector wanted to speak to them in person and ask them to meet her as soon as they could in her office.

10

At about 3:15 in the afternoon of Thursday, 4th December, Rosario Hurtado, instructed by Manuela Vázquez, made two phone calls. The first was to Signora Cremona's cell, but when she did not receive an answer, she sent her a text. The second call was to Rosa Casasaies who responded at once. The agent connected her with the sub-inspector.

"I need a favor," Manuela told Rosa. "I need copies of a couple of students' university files. I am not sure what I am asking for is legal, but I know that until I have a warrant, I cannot access the files myself. If you fax them to me, you'll save me the effort and expedite the process. I think we have a lead. Please take down the names."

"I'm on it," the professor answered. "I'm on my way to the office right now and have nothing to write the names down on, but as I walk there, could you tell me what kind of lead?"

"I believe we have identified the person who was waiting for Laura outside of the TV studios and also the car, an Opel Corsa with a Tarragona license plate," the sub-inspector said. "I would like to know which of Laura's friends live or are from there. Can you help me? Should I send my assistant to meet you? She is a computer whiz. She's even better than Lisbeth in *The Girl with the Dragon Tattoo*; I imagine you've read the book? I am sure she could hack your computers from the station, but that would be totally illegal. If you help us with the information, the thing will only be partly illegal ... we can share the blame."

"Great!" Rosa agreed with a laugh. "So you want me as your accomplice?"

Closing her office door behind her, Rosa sat at her desk and picked up pen and paper.

"OK, spit out the names. Is it a long list?"

"No," Manuela said. "First I want the files of Domenica Arrigo and Marcel Bru, and those of Iliescu and Cremona, in case we have missed some important detail. I also want those of Helen Parker and Vladimir Stoica, the Hungarian student. We have spoken with him by phone and suspect he is lying. He alleges he didn't know Iliescu which contradicts Domenica's statement. As for Helen Parker, as soon as we try to speak with her, she hangs up. This always arouses suspicion."

"This is too much paper to fax to you without people noticing," Rosa said. "I can try to make photocopies which is less noticeable. If you send your agent, besides looking for students from Tarragona, she can bring the copies to you. Let me make it clear that this is private stuff only the students themselves can access. As for the lead, can you name the person you have your eye on?"

"Not yet, because I want Laura's mothers who are on their way to identify that the person getting in the car is their daughter. I think she is, but I've seen her only on TV and in a photograph. Her hair covers part of her face, but you can see her body and her hands. She has a ring on her right hand that she didn't have or didn't show on the TV program and this gives me pause. If the mothers recognize the ring, we'll be sure it's hers. I wouldn't want to appear ridiculous by arresting someone else's friend. You understand, right?"

"Of course," Rosa said. "Things don't need to be complicated any further. I'll go get the files. Tell your assistant to call my cell when she gets here."

★

At five o' clock that evening, the Italian consul's chauffeur stopped the car before the Cerdanyola police station for Signore

Cremona and Hogarth to get out. The sub-inspector showed them to her office, telling them to excuse the inspector who couldn't be there as he'd been called to a meeting elsewhere. Manuela Vázquez offered them a glass of water or if they preferred, a cup of coffee, but she regretted this at once. The muddy ooze from the station's coffeemaker was disgusting; it was just dirty water hyperbolically called coffee. And the women, as they were Italian, must be used to a decent brew. The shortness of funds brought about by the Generalitat's cuts meant that a Nespresso machine would be a superfluous expense.

The nervous women declined both offers. The only thing they wanted was to see the images from the security cameras outside the television studios. Vázquez understood. Her daughter was twenty-one and had been born in May 1987, the same month as the vanished girl, a fact that put her in Clara Cremona's shoes and filled her with empathy.

Manuela Vázquez got the DVD with the tapes and a file from her desk and asked the Signore Cremona-Hogarth to go with her to the audio-visual room, a space with gray walls, like the rest of the station. Whoever had chosen that hue for the color of the offices had meant to emphasize that in these new democratic times, the *mossos* police was ready to admit that all was not black and white. It was advisable to bet on gray, the color of gradation and consensus.

The sub-inspector lowered the blinds and lit a lamp for just a moment, so she could see the projector and switch it on. The security cameras had not gotten much: Laura was leaving the TV station lobby, at the gate she bumped into some people coming in, including a well-known football sportscaster and a middle-aged woman who was later identified by the station as one of the make-up people on the late shift. Then Laura crossed the street and for a few seconds, was hidden behind a bus picking up the guests attending a contest that had just ended. As soon as the bus took off, you could see a young man standing near a poorly parked car, a dark Opel Corsa. With a sudden movement, he got into the driver's seat and opened the passenger door for a young woman. Even though her hair obscured half her face, Clara and Margaret recognized her at once.

"Who is this guy? Do you know? Can you identify him? Will he be brought in?" They both asked at the same time, one in Spanish and the other in English.

"Yes," Manuela Vázquez answered. "We know who it is, we have identified him and as soon as we get the detention order we requested from the judge about an hour ago, we'll bring him in."

"Is it a friend of Laura's?" Clara asked. "Is it Iliescu?"

At that point, the sub-inspector turned on the lights and from the folder she had brought, pulled out the files of Laura's companions that Rosa Casasaies had e-mailed her Monday afternoon, right after Domenica had reported her friend missing. Next to the full names, ID or passport numbers, there were wallet-size photos of each student, the same as the ones on their transcripts and she passed the files on to the mothers for them to have a good look. Then she turned on the projector again, found the spot and zoomed in on the young man waiting for Laura. She rewound the tape a little to show him strolling in front of the television studio before Laura came out. After some time, she asked the ladies to identify him in one of the file photographs.

They didn't have any hesitation this time either and pointed at the picture of Marcel Bru.

11

After Marcel Bru was identified, the Cremona case took a different turn, quite a nasty one for the Autònoma's community since one of its students was now the main suspect. The sub-inspector, however, considered that the security images were insufficient to label Bru as the person responsible for Laura's disappearance. Further proof was needed, even though he had hidden the fact that he had picked up Laura after her interview. Manuela Vázquez wondered why he did not to tell Domenica that he had gone to the TV3 studios to meet Laura. Why was he lying? What did he know about the girl that he did not want to share? And about Iliescu? Of all the school friends of the Romanian, Bru was the one who had most insisted on finding out the truth about his disappearance. The posting of flyers had been his idea. On the other hand, he seemed genuinely worried about what could have happened to Laura. He might have told Domenica that he'd been with Laura and now they were both lying. Why had they stated over and over that when she left the TV studios, Laura had vanished and that they had no other news of her except for the message to Domenica? Did they know where she was and refused to disclose her location?

Manuela Vázquez kept thinking that Domenica was telling the truth and that Bru was lying. She had spoken with the girl twice and found no contradictions in her statements, an important point in her favor. Despite this, however, and despite her belief that Domenica had nothing to do with the disappearance of her friends, Vázquez thought she ought to question her again after she had spoken with Bru and found out how he justified his lies. What had happened after they left TV3? Where did they go? Was Bru the friend Laura was to go out with for a beer? And if that was the case, why did Laura not mention his name in her message to Domenica? "Marcel" was not too long a word, no longer than *amico*, which was the word Laura had typed and "Bru" was even shorter. Young people tailored their text messages for economy of expression, but this case did not seem to fit. The friend must have been someone Domenica did not know; perhaps she'd picked him up at the TV set itself. Depending on what Marcel would say, she decided she would speak with the team of TV technicians. She had already questioned the interviewer and the head of the news program.

This was what Manuela Vázquez kept chewing the cud over. She thought in terms of "chewing the cud" rather than "mulling over" because she preferred the former idiom. She even advised the young agents under her command to imitate cows. "The cows, being ruminants, chew twice what they have swallowed by returning the cud to their mouths," she would tell them. "We must do it as many times as necessary, not just twice, until we are sure that what we'll finally digest is the truth."

Her innate curiosity had led her to try out for the National Police Corps. She was sure that such work would help her develop all she'd learned in college. She was interested in knowing first-hand the mechanics of human behavior and, however unforeseeable or rare, find the why behind it. "Any action," she stated, "even the worst of crimes, has a justification, no matter how wrong, immoral or unnatural it might be. There are no gratuitous acts. There is always a cause that will allow us to understand and then to reject the reasons of the criminal."

★

Agent Rosario Hurtado knocked on the door of Manuela Vázquez's office when the sub-inspector, holding her pot of orchids, was about to go out to water them just enough to keep them happy and make good company. The younger woman had a folder with photocopies of the students' files and the list of those whose home addresses were in or near Tarragona. The sub-inspector told her to wait a second. The water cooler was not very far. She dripped some water onto the soil in the pot and making sure no liquid oozed from underneath it, returned to her office and closed the door behind her.

"I imagine you've been smart enough to keep quiet about Bru," she told the agent. "I suspect Rosa Casasaies has asked not once, but several times who our suspect was."

"Who he was or who she was. She deduced it must be one from the files we requested."

"Let me see Marcel Bru's; I'll write down his data in my notebook. Is he from Tarragona? Too bad we could not see the whole license plate of the car. We'll have to resort to the Traffic Police to identify the owner, but let's not bring them in on this if we can avoid it. Only if Bru refuses to say whose car it is and hinders our investigation."

Marcel Bru was not from Tarragona, the city or the province, and judging from the information in his file, neither were his parents. His home was in Vilanova i la Geltrú, where he'd been born twenty-four years ago on 7th April 1984. In Barcelona, he lived on 66 Carretera de la Bordeta in the Sants neighborhood.

"When do you want us to go get him, sub-inspector?' Rosario asked, looking at her watch. "It's ten after six. When we get to Sants, with the traffic at this time of day, it'll be at least 7 o'clock by the time we get there. I don't think Bru will be home doing his homework at this hour. Perhaps you should go there at 7 in the morning, a more likely time to find him."

"I think you're right. When I was a girl during the Franco years, police went to arrest political dissidents in the early morning. They knocked loudly on the doors, waking all the neighbors, and dragged the suspects out of bed with blows and yells and didn't even let them get dressed. I would not want to imitate that system. My uncle, a union foreman at the SEAT factory, was once taken like that, and even today he hasn't forgiven me for being in the police force…but you're right; the best time to find Bru is probably around seven o' clock or even a little earlier. Are you a morning person?"

"Not really, but I don't mind," Rosario answered. "It'll look good on my record. When should we go? Five instead of seven o' clock?"

"Let's say 6:30," the sub-inspector suggested, looking at her computer screen. 'Meet me on the corner of Carretera de la Bordeta and Àliga. I won't give you a ride because I don't want to be censured. You live in Castelldefels which is not on the way."

Then she picked up the phone and asked: "Is the judge's warrant here? Bring it to me as soon as it arrives." And addressing Rosario, she said: "You can go home now. Tomorrow will be a long day."

12

At 6:30 in the morning, there was already quite a lot of movement on Carretera de la Bordeta, even though it was not yet light. The sky produced nothing but darkness. It was cold. The ground was wet, as if just hosed, thanks to that bone-piercing humidity that so often invades Barcelona. Without street lamps and the brightness of traffic lights and vehicles, it would have been hard to see. But soon the milky light of dawn spread across the skies and an ash-gray and chilly morning emerged, a clear sign that the unusual mild weather of the past week had ended.

The cafés, markets, fruit stands and all the food vendors, the earliest of the shops to function, started to open their doors, most making a metallic racket. Traffic was intensifying. Unmindful of the neighbors sleeping, some drivers honked repeatedly, annoyed by the delivery vans arriving from Mercabarna – the wholesale distribution point for foodstuffs – that obstructed the traffic flow with their delivery stops.

Rosario Hurtado got to her appointment before Manuela Vázquez, at about 6:20 that morning. She looked sleepy and felt cold, but did not dare go into the corner café from which wafted a disgusting smell of cheap grilled cheese. She preferred to wait rather than make Manuela wait. The agent was determined to earn merit points to aid her aspirations for transfer to a station closer to her home as soon as a position would open. She did not want the sub-inspector, who was very punctual, to find her missing at the venue, particularly after getting out of bed so early.

At 6:29 Manuela Vázquez, looking somewhat like a Muslim woman due to the black ankle-length raincoat and the head scarf she had worn to fight the rain that had begun to fall, approached her subordinate: "We've parked in front of Bru's building," she said. "It's very near here. We've brought two cars. Toni Rafà will stay with you as you search the apartment. I will leave with Jordi Quatrecases and the suspect. Yesterday, after you left, I spoke with the inspector. He thought the four of us should come. I imagine he wanted us to have the protection of two men. The guy doesn't know how resourceful we can be, you and I," she looked at Rosario with an air of complicity, "especially at this early hour. He seems to have forgotten you got a Silver in the Olympic marksmanship competition."

Rosario Hurtado rubbed her eyes and smiled. She was a tall and strong young woman from the Navarra region, the daughter of a Civil Guard agent who, in March 1991, had been sent to the Vic precinct a few months before the ETA attack there during which her sister was killed. Given this history, it wasn't hard to imagine family reasons for Rosario to want to join the *mossos*. Besides, she was fond of those American television serials where first-class police agents upheld the rule of law. She wore a locket which contained a lock of hair from her dead sister. Since she wasn't shy to tell the story to whoever would ask or reveal the contents of the locket whenever someone wanted to see what was inside, Rosario was often reputed to be a necrophile. She was aware of this, but didn't care. She thought that as long as she spoke about Núria, as long as her sister was present in her mind, she was somehow bringing her back to life. The sub-inspector preferred Rosario to all other subordinates because she was the most intuitive, not to mention responsible, and was passionate about her work.

The apartment building where Marcel Bru lived was an old one. A plaque on its front indicated it was a 'Rent-control Residence' built in 1957. The main entrance door was unlocked, there was no elevator and the stairs were narrow, steep and dark. The four of them walked up to the third floor and rang the second doorbell. There was no answer. They rang again. The door next to it opened. An old woman in a nightgown asked what they wanted. She thought they had rung for her apartment; she was afraid her son might have met with an accident. Then she told them that her next-door neighbors were a bunch of yahoos who stayed awake at night and slept during the day, and they should keep ringing the doorbell. They did so until they heard footsteps and the door opened. It was a young man in boxer shorts and a tee-shirt.

"We're looking for Marcel Bru," the sub-inspector said.

"He's asleep," the young man said. "And so was I. Shit, it's too early for anything! Come on, come back later."

He tried to close the door, but he hadn't noticed two feet that prevented him. One of the feet, in a reinforced running shoe, was Antoni Rifà's, the other, in a hiking boot, was Rosario Hurtado's. She liked to wear those boots from time to time. They reminded her of the day she first put them on when she was accepted as a Girl Scout in the Pyrenees town where she spent part of her adolescence. The man in the tee-shirt froze.

"Please let us in," Manuela Vázquez said as she showed him her badge. And with a smile she asked mockingly: "Whom do I have the pleasure of speaking to?"

From the way he stared at her, perplexed, it seemed that her polite phrase was not part of his usual vocabulary, and he did not answer. Then, shielded by the agents, she stepped into the corridor which doubled as foyer and in a blunter and colder tone she reserved for those she distrusted, told him: "You must have misunderstood me. I've asked for your name." Then she added: "You will please tell us where Marcel Bru is."

"Hey, not so fast! What did you think? I know your tricks. Are you from the Les Corts station?"

The sub-inspector did not reply. Recently, the newspapers had been full of references to some colleagues from the Les Corts district accused of torturing a suspect.

"First, the search warrant," the young man demanded haughtily. "My father is an attorney and I am a law student."

Manuela Vázquez showed him the judge's order that allowed her to detain Bru and inspect the apartment.

"Your name, sir, or would you rather accompany us?"

"Andreu Ràfols," he answered, and stupidly went on, "Do you want to see my ID?"

Vázquez pointed at Rosario.

"Show it to the agent," she said.

As was their procedure whenever they had to arrest someone or search a place, they positioned themselves. Rifà remained at the door in case the suspect decided to run out. Hurtado walked further into the apartment to see how the place was laid out and figure out if an escape was easy. Only a weak bulb near the door threw light on the corridor with its walls stained with humidity and a ceiling discharging bits of lime dust. It led to a messy living area with a balcony opening to an inside court where the shoes of the inhabitants were airing along a ham bone hanging from a nail. From that balcony, you could jump all the way down to street level. Disorder and squalor dominated the whole place. Dirty dishes were piled up in the kitchen sink and over the stove sat pots and pans with moldy remains of food. It must have been quite a while since a mop had touched the bathroom; the porcelain of the sink and tub was the rabid color of bile and, on top of that hepatic yellow, sat cuttings of the hair and beards of those who groomed themselves facing the rickety mirror over the lavatory.

During the time Rosario Hurtado made her investigation, Manuela Vázquez asked Andreu Ràfols to accompany her to the room where he claimed Marcel Bru slept. The second bedroom belonged to Ràfols and a third to a student of economics who, according to Ràfols, came from the same town as Bru. Bru's bedroom door was ajar. From the bed, trying to sit up, he said in an angry tone: "Fuck, what's going on? I didn't do anything!"

"Get dressed," the sub-inspector ordered, "and step on it. You have to accompany us to the police station."

"I didn't do anything," he protested again. "What the fuck! I need to know why I have to go down to the station with you at 6:30 this fucking morning!"

"It has to do with Laura Cremona's disappearance," said the sub-inspector. "We have proof that you could be implicated in it. Presumably."

"I've done nothing to Laura, nothing."

Bru's bedroom had piles of crumpled clothes on the floor and books and papers strewn over the desk and a lone chair. Tacked to a wall was one of the flyers with Iliescu's picture.

13

While the sub-inspector and agent Quatrecases were taking Marcel Bru to the Cerdanyola police station, the other two mossos remained in the apartment, following orders from their boss. Rosario got some latex gloves from her knapsack and began by looking in the drawers of the bedside table in Bru's bedroom. All she found in them were some used condoms, marijuana roaches, a couple of cigarettes and a pack of chewing gum. She then looked through the desk drawers. There were papers, bills, old pens and some photographs. One showed Bru with his arms around a girl the agent thought was Domenica. Her guess was confirmed when, on the back of another photo with the same girl, she read: "To my dear love, Marcel, from Domenica." A third picture showed Domenica next to Laura. Then, three of just Laura, one of them crumpled and torn.

Rosario picked up her knapsack, which she had hung on the back of the chair, and got out two plastic bags. She put the condoms in one and the photographs in the other and continued her search. She wanted to find Bru's computer, an essential source for leads, but perhaps he didn't have one and used one from the university or went to Internet cafés. She looked in the closet. There was only dirty laundry. She piled the clothes on the floor to find out if was something more interesting among the shirts, socks and underpants, but nothing caught her eye. She then looked under the bed. Old shoes, slippers and a small suitcase. When she opened it, she found a bunch of CDs and some pornographic magazines under a rather smelly towel.

Rosario Hurtado had to go to the kitchen in search for a garbage bag because the ones she had were too small for all that.

★

While Hurtado scoured the room, Antoni Rifà spoke with Bru's roommates. To begin with, he wanted to know how they got along with Bru and how long they had known him. Andreu Ràfols had met Bru at the start of the academic year when he showed up at the apartment after seeing an announcement in his school offering a room for a decent rent. The other student, Oriol Pagès, an economics major, had known him for several years. They came from the same town, had attended the same high school and had rented together the apartment on Carretera de la Bordeta since the previous academic year. They had previously shared it with Marcel's girlfriend, a girl from Girona who studied translation at the Universitat de Vic and with another boy who was not a student, but an accountant for a small plumbing business in the neighborhood. Marcel had broken up with Remei right away and had kicked her out; the accountant left soon after. Pagès told them he was a neat and clean person and could not stand the mess Bru made. They had agreed on taking turns cleaning. Each week, one of them would be in charge, but the accountant claimed he was the only one to do his part, which Pagès said was not quite true. He was also annoyed because the noise they made didn't let him sleep. "When Remei lived with us," he said, "she and Marcel spent all night watching DVDs which they played at top volume."

Since the relationship among the apartment inhabitants offered nothing but trivialities, Rifà moved on to more concrete questions. He began playing the role of a good cop: "I don't think Bru has done anything bad. He seems like a law-abiding citizen. What do you think?"

"He's a good guy," Oriol Pagès replied. "I've known him for years."

Because the agent noticed that Andreu Ràfols was quiet, he asked him point blank what he thought of Bru, though he knew the boy was loath to collaborate with the police who had gotten him out of bed at such an irreverent hour. Despite living in a working-class neighborhood, it could be that Ràfols felt superior. He could be one of those students who never made it to class before noon.

"I have no opinion," Ràfols answered. "But I'd like to know why you have arrested him. What's the charge?"

"Judge's orders," the *mosso* said. "He wants to know what his relationship is with the people from his school who have vanished. Had Iliescu or Cremona ever been to the apartment? Have you ever seen them?"

"No. I've only seen Iliescu's picture. Marcel worked on the flyers. He was very worried." I am sure you need a warrant to interrogate us. It's the law. Besides, there's got to be a lawyer present."

"This is not an interrogation, just a simple conversation," Rifà clarified.

"And conversations consist of questions and answers as you well know, but you have the right to remain silent," Rosario added with a mocking smile.

She had just entered the room and seeing that they would get nothing of value from Bru's roommates and that Rifà had not gone about it too smartly, she told him she had everything she needed and they could leave.

★

On their way to the Cerdanyola station, Marcel Bru insisted that since he did not know anything about Laura, he did not see why he'd been shoved out of bed and handcuffed.

"What the fuck are you hoping to get from arresting me?" He shouted.

"We want to know the truth," the sub-inspector answered him, "nothing else. We believe you have not been telling us everything. And that is why we want to ask you some questions with the judge's permission, to be certain, when we arrive in Cerdanyola. You can be sure of one thing: we could never detain you without a warrant."

From that moment on, Bru stopped protesting, closed his eyes and leaned his head on the back of the seat, pretending to be asleep or maybe he did fall asleep because when they arrived, Manuela Vázquez had to shake him to get him to move. Then she took him to a room where an agent frisked him, removed everything from his pockets, fingerprinted him and took mug shots. Vázquez asked him if he wanted a cup of coffee which might help his alertness as he waited for the lawyer. "I think you ought to be awake," she told him.

Inspector Martín González wanted to see the suspect. He asked Bru whether they had read him his rights and warned him that the best he could do was to cooperate with the authorities. Marcel Bru did not open his mouth, not even to acknowledge he had read quite carefully article 17 of the Constitution and article 520 of the Criminal Code.

"Very well," the inspector said. "You can refuse to answer; you can wait to do so in front of the judge, but the more obstacles you put up, the more implicated you'll appear in Laura Cremona's disappearance."

14

It wasn't until about noon after they told him they had the
security camera tapes that Marcel Bru admitted that he *had*
gone to pick up Laura Cremona at the TV3 studios in a
car borrowed from his cousin. Peppering every phrase with a
string of "fucks," he confessed that after leaving the studios, the
two of them went for drinks to a bar in the Raval. Toward two
o' clock in the morning, he had taken her back to Bellaterra.
He left her at the university's Vila, about fifty steps from her
building. Laura wanted to turn in early; she had sent a text to
Domenica saying she wouldn't be late. In the text she didn't
mention his name; she simply wrote: "a friend," so as not to
upset the jealous Domenica who was still stuck on him even
though they'd broken up.

"Were you attracted to Laura?" Inspector Martínez González
asked.

"Fuck, man! We were just friends."

"She paid no attention to you, did she? She had a thing
for Iliescu, but when he disappeared, you thought she was fair
game, right?"

Bru did not reply. Manuela Vázquez, who was present at the
interrogation, noticing that he blushed but kept quiet, answered
for him, choosing words that would lead him to incriminate
himself: "There can be no doubt, Inspector, the presumed
suspect responsible for Laura's disappearance fancied her. But
she ignored him, therefore ..."

"I've done nothing to Laura, I swear. Fuck! I told you I
dropped her off around 2 o'clock in the morning in front of

her place at the Vila. Fuck! Then I went to the Zona Hermètica in Sabadell where my cousin was waiting. I needed to return his car on time because he had to go to Tarragona on Saturday to see his parents. I had to stand in line outside the disco which was very crowded and I sat with him and his friends until six o' clock. Then I returned by train to Barcelona."

"Domenica swears that Laura never made it back home," the sub-inspector said. "And that you are responsible for her disappearance." She picked up the receiver to ask for Domenica to be shown in.

The girl's eyes were red from crying. She had also been brought over that morning, but at a more decent hour, after Rosario had arrived in Cerdanyola with the photos she had found in Bru's room. Vázquez wanted her to explain their relationship which, judging from appearances, was more than a mere friendship. She showed her the tapes that proved that Laura and Marcel had seen each other and asked her if she knew about it and if so, why she hadn't told them. As soon as she set foot in the room, Domenica shouted at Bru: "Liar! Pig! Why did you hide from us that you spent the night with Laura? What did you do to her that you don't want us to know?"

Bru avoided her gaze. He kept staring at his handcuffs with bowed head and said nothing. The girl was sobbing.

"I see," the inspector said, "Domenica also thinks you're lying." Then in an energetic tone of voice he shot: "Where's Laura? What did you do with her that night? Why don't you tell us now in front of Domenica? At what time did you say you dropped her off?"

Without raising his head, Bru answered,

"Around two o' clock. Maybe a little later."

"Did you get out of the car to walk her to her door?"

"I did not. And fuck, I regret it because then I would be sure that the one responsible for her disappearance is Domenica. Domenica hated Laura. You didn't know that, did you? Do her parents know? People should know."

"He lies!" spat out Domenica. "All he says are lies."

Marcel Bru flashed a nasty smile and cast her a derisive glance over his eyeglasses. Manuela Vázquez tried to calm Domenica and asked her to accompany her to her office.

She closed the door, offered her some water and gave her a minute to collect herself before she asked: "Are you sure, Domenica, that Laura never made it back home? What were you doing at two o' clock in the morning? Were you home?"

"Yes, I was."

"Sleeping?"

"No, not yet. A friend had dropped by and we were chatting and listening to music."

"Perhaps Laura came in without you noticing. Where were the two of you, in the living room or in your bedroom?"

"In the bedroom."

"Then it is likely that you didn't hear her."

"I am sure Laura never made it back. Her room was exactly as she left it on Friday when she went to Barcelona. When I went in on Saturday before three o' clock her bed was made and on it were the leggings and sweater she had thought of wearing for the TV interview before she finally decided to wear something else. I know this because, before leaving on Friday, she asked me what looked better."

"She could have left early on Saturday without you noticing it. At what time did your friend leave?"

"Saturday morning, around ten o' clock."

"What's his name?"

"I don't want to involve him in all this…Neither he nor I have anything to do with Laura's disappearance."

★

Manuela Vázquez understood the girl's reluctance to reveal whom she had spent the night with, but she needed to know. He could be an important witness and she would consider bringing him in. She had asked Domenica to meet her at the station and the girl had come there right away without complaining. No one considered her a suspect, even though her affair with Marcel Bru made her relationship with Laura more complicated. Perhaps Domenica wasn't telling the whole truth. Perhaps she hated Laura as Bru alleged and didn't dare show it. It could be that deep down, she was happy about the disappearance. And if Bru was involved in the disappearance, she might feel avenged. As the saying went, there was but one short step between love and hate. The sub-inspector remembered her ex-husband, but quickly shoved the memory aside. "Concentrate on your job," she told herself and again addressed the distressed person sitting in front of her: "You've done great so far, Domenica. Don't botch it up now. We need to know the name of the person who was at your place last Friday night and also tell us about your relationship with Marcel Bru. We all thought you were just friends. You can start wherever you prefer."

"I got involved with Marcel when I arrived in Barcelona. I liked him. I liked to hear him talk, I found him cute. But then Laura came. I introduced them, we went out, the three of us and he got a thing for her without telling me…Laura told me. But she couldn't stand him. Only when Iliescu vanished did she pay any attention to Marcel because he was being very nice, very helpful…"

"Do you still love him?" Manuela asked. "Are you fond of him?"

"No. Not anymore," the girl answered quickly and broke into tears.

"Do you believe he could be capable of killing Laura?"

The girl nodded with teary eyes and a running nose.

"Who was with you Friday night?"

"I went to the campus hotel bar to see Laura on television because we don't have a TV in the apartment. It is not true I hate her as Marcel says; I love her. I am envious of her, that's all; she is prettier and smarter, she is more popular than me with guys. At the bar I met Professor Bellpuig. He was by himself. We saw the program together and then he accompanied me home and asked me if he could come up."

15

What the police found most striking was the fact that Marcel Bru had not mentioned from the start that he had been with Laura on the night of her disappearance. That Laura had not told Domenica that the friend meeting her was Bru made some sense, but for him to hide the encounter made no sense whatsoever if he had broken up with Domenica. According to his lawyer, the reason for Bru's silence was fear: he was afraid of being incriminated if he told the police that he had accompanied Laura to the campus at night, just the two of them, and in a car that wasn't his. It was now clear that his secrecy was a big mistake and he was paying for it. But the lawyer was sure he could come up with a valid alibi and therefore recommended that he employ all his senses to reconstruct moment by moment and step by step, every movement on the night of 28th November, from the time he picked Laura up until he went home to bed at eight o' clock in the morning on Saturday. If he could convince the police that he was innocent, he could go home. Otherwise, he might continue in detention even past the regulatory seventy-two hours because the judge would decree jail time.

From the TV3 studios where they went first, Bru led Rosario Hurtado and Antoni Rifa all the way to the bars in the Raval where he claimed he had been with Laura after they had walked around the neighborhood. The first of the bars was the Robador 23 on the street of the same name and the other one, where they stopped at around 12:30, was the Kentucky on Carrer Arc del Teatre. Both spots were crowded and, much as he swore they'd been there, it would be highly unlikely that anyone would remember seeing them, even though Laura was quite spectacular and had not removed her makeup from the television studio.

Bru had chosen the Robador 23 because he'd been told that some guys he knew would be playing there. At least one of them was from Vilanova and for a while they had been more or less friends. But Bru realized quickly that he had the wrong day or the wrong band, but because Laura thought it amusing that to enter the bar you had to ring a bell, even though there was nothing clandestine going on inside, they stayed a little while.

When Bru and the officers went there, the place was less crowded. Rosario went to the counter. There was some flamenco music on, her favorite, she was happy to point out. Then she flashed her badge and asked the bartender if he'd been on duty last Friday night and if he could remember the young man who was with her.

"None of us have Fridays off," he answered. "The place was full and we could barely keep up with the orders...I'm sorry." And then, addressing Bru, added: "If by recognizing you, I could help you, I'd like to say yes."

Rosario and Marcel smiled. The agent produced a picture of Laura from her bag and showed it to the bartender.

"Does this jog your memory?" Rosario asked. "Can you recall this face? It's Laura, the young woman who disappeared a week ago." Pointing at Bru, she added: "He says he was here with her."

"Wow, she's hot! But, sorry, no. What did you say happened to her?"

"She vanished near her place in Bellaterra," Rosario answered. "No one has seen her since the wee hours of last Saturday."

"Hmm, sounds bad; so much time has gone by without any sign of life!"

At the Kentucky, where according to Bru, they had spent more time because they were lucky enough to be able to sit at the bar, none of the waiters could place Laura or Marcel.

But then, Bru recalled a detail that could prove that he, at least, had been there that night at that time: a young woman had collapsed from lipothymia. She was there with a group of Italians and that's why Laura walked up to speak to them. The waiter also remembered the fainting and asked to be shown Cremona's picture again and decided that yes, Marcel and his friend *had* been there.

With somewhat lifted spirits, Bru told Rosario, the only agent whom he did not despise, that he had another proof of having been downtown and walking around that area at the hours he had mentioned. He had left the car at the Boqueria parking garage, a place that had security cameras and since they trusted such technology, he urged them, fuck, to request the tapes from the garage management.

The agent asked Bru what floor he had parked on and then told Antoni Rifà, who drove the mossos car, to go to the Boqueria and proceed as Bru suggested. According to the boy, he had parked the Opel Corsa on Level One, not far from the exit stairs, but understandably, could not give further details since he never imagined anything of importance resulting from that night.

It was already dark when they left Barcelona, the traffic much denser than it had been in the morning. Everyone in that car was tired, having risen early. The police knew that Bru's fatigue was an advantage for them and that perhaps, when they got to campus and approached the Vila housing units, he would give up and tell them finally what had happened. But nothing like that came about. Without any hesitation, the boy told the driver the route they had followed that night and the spot, some fifty meters from Laura's front door, where she had gotten off. But he could offer no other proof that he had, in fact, dropped her off there.

16

On Friday morning, a retiree who was walking his dog along the path which traversed the woods from Ciutat Badia and ended at the parking lot of the School of Letters made a macabre discovery. In his statement, Pere Ribas i Tarongí claimed that it was the dog that made the discovery. "Bernat is smarter than many people I know and I let him off the leash when I can," said the old man. "He suddenly bolted from my side, dashed to a certain spot and began to bark near a crevice between two boulders, as if calling me. Since I am old and creaky and rheumatism has declared war on my joints, you can imagine I don't move very fast and walking is hard for me. That's why I ignored him at first, sat down on the cane stool I always carry with me when I go for a stroll and waited for the dog to return to my side instead of trekking to see what he had found that day. Bernat hasn't lost his fine sense of smell, he was an excellent hunter when young. Lately, he's lost energy, just like me and it is hard for him now to run to the partridges I down or set the thrushes flying, but he still leaps up to tell me he's found a hedgehog or a hare warren."

Pere Ribes decided to wait for his dog's return, mumbling curses at him, blaming him for old-age glumness, obstinacy and disobedience. From where he was waiting, sitting on his portable stool, he could hear, but not see him. At last, he got up to fetch the barking Bernat, fearing he was stuck somewhere. He had heard about spring traps some sons of bitches had set in that area to catch rabbits. When he got to the spot, he saw Bernat looking at him reproachfully.

"With the years you've become more and more idiotic," the dog seemed to tell him. "I've been barking and barking for an hour and you're not paying attention."

"You're right, you're right," said Pere Ribes, "but you don't seem to see you've aged too, old dog. Of course, since you don't shave, you can't see yourself in the mirror. Come, let's go, it's about to rain. I thought you'd hurt yourself."

Pere tried to put the leash back on his dog, but the animal jerked his head to avoid it and ran to a crevice in the stone, some three or four meters further and stopped there, still barking. When he had been sitting on that great invention, the cane stool, the old man had sensed a weird smell; this stench was now becoming more intense with every step and he imagined it would be from some dead animal in the pile of junk that filthy people dump.

"Any day now," he said to the dog, "there will be no woods, just garbage dumps and there's no point in your getting mad and barking it to the authorities; they pay no heed. Come, let's go, move, you darned dog!"

But Bernat did not obey and then Pere looked inside the crevice and saw to his horror, under some torn garbage bags, probably gnawed by field rats, a hand with a large band on its ring finger that he thought belonged to a woman.

"Good Lord!" he said out loud, "Lord in Heaven!" And he patted his pockets to find out what he already suspected: he hadn't brought his cell phone and he thought of his wife scolding him for having forgotten it once again.

Pere Ribes i Tarongí realized he was closer to the university than to his house and so went to the university campus, just five minutes up the hill. He imagined that someone there would let him call 112. He tried to convince his dog to abandon his discovery.

"Don't worry, Bernat, you'll get the credit," he told the animal. "I'll tell everyone. Poor girl...oh Lord, this must be one of those girls the mafia abandoned down there, near the highway. Perhaps they killed her because she was trying to escape."

★

The first person Pere Ribes ran into was a building manager who had just gotten out of her car at the Letters parking lot. In an agitated state, the old man told her what he had found and asked her to let him call the police. The woman invited him to walk with her to the school and there he could call campus security.

When the 112 operator got in touch with the Sabadell police, in whose jurisdiction the discovered body would fall, they had already heard about the case from the Cerdanyola station. Dolors Adrover, trembling, had requested Professor Casasaies to telephone Manuela Vázquez to go to the spot in the woods. Vázquez had contacted her colleagues in Sabadell; being a larger force, they had better means and personnel than the Cerdanyola police and were in charge of homicides, as Ribes's discovery seemed to be.

The first to get to the Letters parking lot were two policemen who happened to be patrolling the campus area. From the lot, they followed the dog and its owner to the spot where the discovery had been made. Had it not been for the hand popping up from the garbage heap, the whole thing might have been overlooked. Or rather, it would have surfaced much later, since Manuela Vázquez had put in a request for agents to organize a search around the campus. But this would not have been the area she would have investigated first. She aimed to check the vicinity of the Vila apartments where Bru told them he had dropped Laura off the night of her disappearance, a place to the northwest, abutting the ritzy part of the Vallès region, not the working-class area to the southeast.

When Manuela Vázquez and Rosario Hurtado got there, the Sabadell mossos had already enclosed the area and shooed away students, professors, administrators and staff who, expectant and silent, had approached the spot. They were now clustering on the parking lot, awaiting news of the victim's identity. Rosa Casasaies felt her pulse quicken and a cold sweat breaking out over her whole body. She surprised herself by praying to God – she who boasted of her agnosticism – for the body not be Laura's or that of any student or any person having to do with the Autònoma. She much preferred the hypothesis of the old man talking to his dog, who said it must be a wretched prostitute, an immigrant from Eastern Europe.

About five hundred meters down from Casasaies, the sub-inspector collected pieces of the garbage bags and some branches covering the corpse. If it were Laura's, she didn't want to imagine the tragedy it would be for the Signore Cremona. She always tried for the sake of her mental health not to get emotionally involved in her cases, but surprisingly, Laura's case really got to her: she felt moved to the core. She empathized with the mothers' desolation as she thought of her own daughter Sònia and she felt guilty for having been so wrong in her suppositions. Until Bru's arrest, she had considered Laura's disappearance rather unimportant.

As the agents pulled away the debris with which the perpetrator or perpetrators had hidden the body, there were growing signs that the shared wishes of Rosa Casasaies and Manuela Vázquez would not come true. The body they found seemed to be wearing the same clothes – now all torn, dirty and wet – that Laura Cremona had worn on the night of her disappearance as Vázquez had noted. She lay in a fetal position and her stockings were in tatters. The tight blue bodice with printed figures, a Custo design, was ripped at the level of her breasts. The beautiful face of the living Laura, her skin enchantingly luminous, had become an obscene mask because of exposure and putrefaction that no longer belonged to her. It was the private and exclusive property of death, just like all her other body parts, except for her missing right earlobe, which seemed to have been gnawed off by some animal rather than rent by her murderer. There were no traces of blood anywhere on her body. A kind of *foulard* or handkerchief was knotted tight around her neck.

"It looks like," Manuela Vázquez said to Rosario Hurtado, who was also quite shaken, "she died from suffocation by compression of the throat."

A few minutes before the judge ordered the removal of the body and the medical examiner took it to the Hospital Clínic in Barcelona, Inspector Manuel González arrived with Marcel Bru. He wanted to see the reaction of the presumed perpetrator before letting go of the case. Since there was a murder now, the matter could no longer fall to the Cerdanyola station under his command, but to that of Sabadell, a change that would allow him to travel with his mind at rest to Buenos Aires to attend the wedding of his eldest son to an Argentinian woman.

Bru was petrified at the sight of Laura's body. He tried covering his face with his handcuffed hands as he kept saying in a low, heart-wrenching voice: "I didn't do it, I didn't do it, I didn't do it, fuck!" Then he burst into tears.

"Go ahead, cry all you want and start to repent," Martínez González told him. And, as if he hadn't heard the repeated protests of innocence, he added: "You'll be better off confessing. All your alibis stop here."

17

Sub-Inspector Vázquez asked the Italian consul to inform Laura's mothers that the girl's body had been found. Neither she nor Rosa Casasaies, who had more dealings with the ladies than any other professor from the Autònoma, felt ready to break the news to them. She knew the consul could not decline, however uncomfortable he felt about the task.

Dante Braccalente, who had just arrived in his office, decided not to telephone Signore Cremona-Hogarth, much less send them a fax or an e-mail, which were his usual modes of communication, but rather pay them a visit right away and tell them face-to-face, before they heard from anyone else.

On his way toward the Bellaterra hotel, where the mothers were staying as a courtesy from the Autònoma's rector, the consul pondered the best way to break the news to them. He tried to think of phrasing that would do the least damage, but could not think of any and wondered if style really mattered in a case like this. The reality the ladies had to face was so horrible, so monstrous, that it would seem almost frivolous to dress it up with any of the pretty phrases that were his stock-in-trade. There were no terms in Italian or in any of the languages he knew to signify the state in which people who had lost a child felt. He tried to call to memory a line or two from his repertoire of Italian poets that could help him and he recalled some lines from Poliziano, addressed, he thought, to Giuliano de Medici on the occasion of the death of Simonetta Vespucci, a young and beautiful woman like Laura. The consolation that it was better to die young might work for oneself, but it was the worst tragedy for the parents. *Simonetta, il vostro passo di velluto. E il vostro sguardo di vergine violata*...but no, oh no, the verse couldn't be Poliziano; it must be Dino Campana, a poet who went mad and died in an asylum in the thirties.

"*Dio mio, per Baco*," he burst out loud, "was she raped?"

"Were you talking to me, sir?" His chauffeur asked, although he was used to hearing the consul speak to himself.

"No, nothing. I've to make a call. Please lower the volume of the radio."

Dante Braccalente phoned the sub-inspector and asked her if Laura had been raped. She told him they didn't know, the body appeared with underwear on, a positive sign among all that horror, but that the medical examiner would have to verify it and the family would be informed that she would let them know in person, but for the moment, she would rather not guess. The forensic department had taken plenty of samples.

"Excuse me, Consul, I know you'll do great. I mean, you'll tell the mothers in the best way possible, but for the moment, please say nothing of her gnawed ear. You know, I can't get this out of my head."

It was true. Better not to mention that detail, which had killed Dante's appetite, a rare occurrence, even more so today when he had made reservations at the Via Veneto restaurant. He was to have dinner with the Mexican consul, a great friend with whom he shared the opinion that in Barcelona, consuls ought to be considered on par with ambassadors. He might need to reschedule.

"You could insist that the killer – the presumed killer – has been arrested," added the sub-inspector. "It might be a small consolation."

"Consolation, my eye!" he thought. "And it has to be me who tells them! Who knows if this won't bring me bad luck, especially now that I thought I was becoming their friend?"

It was almost noon when the consul arrived at the Bellaterra and asked for Signore Cremona-Hogarth, undecided whether it would be best to go up to their room or meet them in the lobby. He opted to let them choose. But the ladies were not in their room. He then thought he'd gone about the whole thing in the wrong way from the start. Before going to Bellaterra, he should have made sure they were there and let them know of his visit. Now he was forced to look for them and realized that he'd have to tell them the news by phone, after all. With his most mournful voice, as soon as Signora Cremona answered her cell, he said: "I can't tell you how sorry I am, *signora*. You don't know how bad I feel about having to give you this bad news. This morning Laura has been found dead."

There was a silence on the other end. The consul could not tell whether Signora Cremona had fainted or had had a heart attack. He called again, but a tinny voice informed him that the number was unavailable or out of range. Not knowing whether to stay at the hotel or go back to his office, the consul telephoned the sub-inspector. He should have asked where Laura's mother was before saying anything, he should have gone to meet her, help her, console her…he felt despondent.

"Don't worry," Manuela told him, "Signora Cremona and Signora Hogarth are here. They were at the door when you called. The inspector is now with them in his office. Come to the station. I am sure you'll be of help."

★

The inspector and the sub-inspector ushered the ladies into the former's office, which was a bit larger, but furnished, functional and also with gray walls. Martínez González confirmed the news. The ladies had rushed to Cerdanyola directly on hearing at the hotel that a girl had been found dead near the campus. The inspector offered to put them in touch with the psychologist's office for, in cases like this one, it would be available to them, but the women refused. Nothing seemed to assuage their wretchedness. Not even learning that the judge had denied bail to the presumed murderer or the certainty that he would pay for what he had done.

Signora Cremona, staring at the wall in a kind of catatonic state, said nothing. She seemed far away. She didn't even react when the inspector's phone alarm made a frightful whistling noise meant to remind him that it was 12:30 p.m., and along with his third cup of coffee for the day, he should also take a pill for hypertension. Mrs. Hogarth, however, her eyes red from crying, asked to see the girl's body as she had been identified only from photographs and no relative had verified the identity. She was desperately clinging to the hope that the body was not Laura's.

18

At noon on Friday 5th December, Rosario Hurtado had not yet left the Bellaterra woods. The forensic team, outfitted in white overalls, masks and latex gloves, as if they were about to board a spaceship, were gathering as many samples as they could, even though they knew that the garbage under which the body had been hidden, made it difficult to find reliable leads. Hurtado, in her mossos police uniform, scouted the area to see if she could find any of Laura's belongings in some nook or scattered among the fallen leaves. That wasn't her job; she was supposed to make sure no one came near the cordoned-off area, but as some of her colleagues were already making sure the accesses to the campus were under control, she decided she was not needed there and thought she would use the time to help with the search for evidence.

Like all the corpses Hurtado had seen in her short five-year police career, Laura's was barefoot. She could not tell if that recurring detail impressed her more than any other; her favorite pastime was to go window-shopping for shoes. Even though she often wore hiking boots, she thought that true elegance was shown when choosing footwear. She could recall the shoes Laura had worn for the interview – beautiful gray and black high heels. She thought they could be lying there somewhere because whether she'd been forced to walk around the place or been dragged there once dead, she would most likely have lost them.

For her television appearance, Laura had worn a vest over her bodice. Rosario had admired the knit with ribbing made of a silvery dark-gray thread, with a light sheen. She might have lost the vest while the murderer was dragging her, leaving fingerprints on it. She was also on the lookout for Laura's bag, although she had no image of it, and what might be inside: perhaps a cell phone to shed light on what had happened, her keys and wallet. Rosario Hurtado suspected that whoever had killed Laura had done so elsewhere. If it had been Bru, he probably transported her in his cousin's car to the Letters parking lot and from there, on foot, to the spot where she'd been found, trying to bury the corpse in that secluded spot. He must have dragged her; Hurtado thought it unlikely that he had carried her on his shoulder, all 500 meters from the parked car to the crevice where she'd been found. But to know for sure, Hurtado would have to wait for the medical examiner's report and also for the analyses of the forensic department. The last person to see her alive had been Bru, but Rosario had doubts he'd been the murderer. It could be that he wasn't lying about this point and the killer was someone else, someone now walking freely on campus: another student, a professor, one of the many construction workers or a neighbor. The university campus bordered a housing development project site.

When she was a student, she had been taught that murderers and rapists usually kill or rape not very far from their homes, and in some cases, according to Professor David Cauter's theories, the place of residence is equidistant from the two furthest places of activity. Perhaps, the murderer had killed Iliescu before and his body could also be found in these woods.

If she were in command, she would immediately ask for reinforcements to carry out an in-depth search of the place. She had a hunch that the Romanian's body was also buried there. She felt a shudder of apprehension at the thought. Why would anyone wish the death of these two students? What had they done to provoke the killing instincts of their assassin? Was it a crime of passion – the "love that kills," as in the novels her grandmother read – and Bru, the perpetrator?

A bird taking flight from a branch made Rosario, who had been looking at the ground, raise her eyes to the sky, a whitish expanse, bloated like a pregnant belly, just like it was yesterday and the day before. The mild weather had clearly ended. She remained at the spot for a bit, gazing at the overcast sky and thinking about Laura's last moments, wondering if she had been afraid – her roommate had said she was easily frightened – if she'd been raped before being killed, if she had met a quick death or had to suffer.

But she soon looked down again, and continued her search, moving away from the spot where her colleagues worked, descending toward Ciutat Badia. She looked carefully at the bushes and fallen leaves, finding nothing of interest. Suddenly, not far from the highway, she heard the rustle of steps behind her. When she turned around, she saw no one. She kept on walking, thinking that her apprehension made her misinterpret the sounds of the woods as the noise of an approaching person. But again, she was certain someone was following her, stopping whenever she stopped, hiding from view. The tree branches, thick in spots, almost entirely blocked the weak light of the cloudy day. The sun, ailing or lazier than usual, seemed determined not to show up. It could be that the dawn's alarm bell had been too faint and so, the light was now misty, murky, precarious.

If indeed someone was stalking her, Rosario thought, it must be one who knew the area well to be able to hide so opportunely and invisibly. But if what she heard was truly the noise of footsteps and not just the rustle of leaves stirred by intermittent gusts of wind or field rats or moles, why was that person tailing her? To attack her? To challenge the police who were some three or four hundred meters away? Was Iliescu's or Laura's killer following her? She hid. Crouching, she checked if her cell phone worked, but it was out of range, a fact that made her more nervous. She might not have resorted to the phone, but knowing that in a dangerous situation she could not reach her colleagues unnerved her even more. With fear in her bones, she reached for the holster to ensure she had her gun and that if necessary she could use it. She was now concentrating on the noises, trying to survey the area behind her. Being a very good shot comforted her, but she didn't want to shoot a mere swish of leaves or fire up in the air for that would make her companions rush to her aid. She didn't want to look like a little girl calling for help or firing her gun simply because she had a panic attack. No way. She couldn't show that much weakness. Martínez González would be quick to say that such things didn't happen to men or, if they did, it was because they were herky-jerky, and Rosario refused to admit to being inferior or a less able and courageous police agent just because she was a woman. She was, nevertheless, regretting her foolishness for attempting a search all by herself.

For a few minutes, she heard nothing. She decided to turn around and go back up and drew her weapon. "If he's hiding and sees me with gun in hand, he will lose his desire to chase me, he'll think that I am chasing him," she mused. She had climbed some twenty meters, toward the path that led to the cordoned-off area, when she again heard the noise behind her and wondered how it could be possible that three minutes earlier the footsteps had approached from the opposite side. Perhaps it wasn't one but two people who wanted to frighten her, perhaps Laura's killers had been two people, not one. Didn't they say that criminals always returned to the site of the crime? She fired her gun in the air, ready to quickly aim at a concrete spot if necessary. She saw no one. At that very moment, she felt a blow to her head and fell. Her colleagues found her five minutes after having heard the shot. She was unconscious and had an enormous gash on the back of her head.

19

After the discovery of Laura Cremona's body, the judge ordered Marcel Bru to be locked up without bail, even though the young man kept insisting he was not guilty of her death and stubbornly repeated he had dropped her off, alive and well, some fifty paces from her apartment. But the fact that he had no alibi hindered any belief in his innocence. No witness could verify that he stood in a long queue between two and three o' clock in the morning of last Friday, while his friends said they had seen him at the disco at four o' clock. To make the police even more suspicious, he had finally admitted that before Laura had appeared on television, they had made love at his place.

Now, guilt or no guilt, everything depended on the forensic examiner establishing the time of Laura's death and some witness testifying that Bru was not with the girl at the time. The judge also decreed the indictment to be kept secret, which suited the academic authorities. The judge's ruling would help lessen the media interest in the case – with no fresh news, the media would stop talking about it – and would also help recover the calm so necessary for life at the university which was unaccustomed to tragedies of such magnitude.

The Rector Office, by means of an online announcement, addressed to everyone – students, faculty, administrative and service personnel – called for a day of mourning with the suspension of all academic activities to be held on Tuesday the 9th, the first day of classes since Monday was the Feast of the Immaculate Conception, a countrywide holiday. At the

School of Letters, the dean, after her second valium for the day and after offering one to Rosa Casasaies who wouldn't stop crying, chaired an emergency meeting with her team in a more serene mood than she had shown on previous days; since the culprit had been caught, she didn't think she needed to worry. Poor Laura's friend, Constantinu Iliescu, had yet to be found. According to information from the police received that very morning, Marcel Bru kept denying he knew anything about him. But everything seemed to suggest that the testimony of the presumed killer was unreliable; perhaps Bru had eliminated him since he was the obstacle that prevented him from getting close to Laura. What the dean had noticed, as had the other professors, was the way Bru had been ogling the girl.

The vice-dean for Academic Affairs, who did not get along too well with the dean because she thought he had botched the conflict of the anti-Bologna occupiers, interrupted her to state it was premature to condemn anyone.

The dean replied she was not condemning, only suggesting. Then her colleague added what some were speculating by the water coolers: Marcel Bru was a scapegoat, not the killer. There was nothing better than a propitiatory victim to re-establish as soon as possible the rotten order academic life was based on.

The reference to the rotten order offended Dolors Adrover and the meeting which was meant to reach a consensus on how to organize some sort of memorial for the deceased Erasmus scholar, ended as a free-for-all, each member blaming the others.

It was the anti-Bologna protesters, still occupying the School of Letters, who most emphatically and bluntly defended the theory that Bru was a scapegoat and they spread the sentiment among the students attending that afternoon's assembly – a greater number of them than previously, eager for news of the events that the mid-day news programs had publicized. After all, the occupiers, simply because they stayed at the university day and night, were likely to have better information than the rest of the student body staying off campus.

During that afternoon assembly, the occupiers added to their general denunciation of the Bologna plan; they protested that Iliescu's disappearance was of interest to no one. Unmindful that it was chance that had led to the discovery of Laura's body, they alleged that the fact that his body had not yet been found was due simply to lack of interest, as he had also vanished on a Friday on his way to Bellaterra, making it more likely that he was murdered on the same day. After all, despite earning an Erasmus, Iliescu was a mere immigrant from Eastern Europe. If no one pressured or bribed the police, there would be no results. One of the proposals advanced at the assembly called for organizing search parties to comb the campus surroundings to find out if Iliescu's body had also been dropped there like Laura's. But they were fearful of clashing with the mossos – "the curs" as they called them. Knowing that since that morning, as soon as Laura's corpse had surfaced, the mossos were roaming the campus and when outside it, gave themselves more jurisdiction than they legally possessed, the assembled students concluded that none of the occupiers should take part in the search; the police might see a chance to jail them. They asked the students who had not moved into the university to form teams to look for Iliescu, whom they knew, or so they said, to be one of them. They surely referred to the fact that he was from Eastern Europe, from one of the communist countries still admired and defended by many of the occupiers and not to the fact that he had had a hard life and managed to become a student by dogged exertion.

The occupiers were not alone in their eagerness to find Iliescu; besides the police and Interpol, Marcel Bru's family was also keen on finding him. At about 6 o'clock that very evening, finding out that the Brus ran a children's clothing shop on Vilanova's Carrer Major, the journalists, although fearing they would find the store closed, risked going there in the hope of getting statements from the parents of the main suspect. It would improve their ratings. Yet the Brus, despite their distress, kept their doors open. They felt neither they nor any one in their family had anything to hide. They kept saying the police were wrong; Marcel was innocent, he could have never done anything like that.

Marcel's mother was the one who insisted with convincing stubbornness that if she was sure of one thing, it was that her son hadn't done it and she accused Iliescu. If Iliescu didn't show up, it was because he was the one who was guilty, he was Laura's killer.

"What proof do you have?" A journalist from one of most popular Spanish TV evening talk shows asked her.

She simply added that it could have been Iliescu or anyone else, except Marcel. She, who had given birth to him, nursed him, watched over him when he was ill, swore she was dead sure of her son's innocence.

20

Late in the morning of that Friday, 5th December, a time that had tragically marked the lives of Laura Cremona's mothers and Marcel Bru's parents, a special body of the mossos was hunting for evidence near the path leading from the Letters parking lot to Ciutat Badia, hoping to catch the perpetrator of the blow that had left Rosario Hurtado unconscious for about twenty minutes.

Agent Hurtado, still under observation in the Sabadell hospital, could provide no information about her assailant. All she could tell them was that she never got to see anyone, that all she heard were footsteps. She did not confess – this would go against her interests, for she'd be thought unbalanced – that when she came to the hospital's emergency room, she had a feeling that her attacker had been some kind of monster like the ogre her Castilian grandmother would tell her when she was a child and refused to go to bed. Tall, much taller than the cross at the gates of the village in El Bierzo where her grandmother lived, the ogre roamed the roads to snatch sleepless or disobedient children. The fiend would grab the children by the neck with just two fingers and take them away unseen, so nobody could help them, for he had the power to become invisible and go through walls. Rosario had believed the story since no one had ever seen the ogre, although they heard him as he stalked through fallen leaves in the woods next to grandmother's house where Rosario and her siblings spent their holidays.

Today, as she had dropped to the ground from the blow, Rosario had the sensation that the monster approached her clad in a long dark cape and laughed at her with a harsh, hollow laugh which she could still hear from time to time. She told the attending doctors that at times she heard whistling in her ears and at other times she felt them obstructed, but she did not tell them of the dark noise she had noticed as that of bellows stoking the fire.

Her companions didn't take long to scrutinize those dismal woods, a rather small space where devastated nature fought against pollution and the invasion of a number of things – rusty appliances, all kinds of garbage and dirty shreds of plastic that stubbornly kept their hold on the place through rain and storms. It had been quite a while now since some landscape assassins had turned the woods into a dump.

Further down the slope, next to the highway and over some land owned by those who had sold the fields that became the campus, rose a number of sheds, some of which still shielded the tools farmers used to glean from meager lots of some five hundred square meters the paltry tomatoes or puny lettuces the seasons offered. Some of those abandoned shacks with sagging roofs and missing doors sheltered vagrants, almost always alone, especially during the summer months.

Suspecting one such tramp might have been the perpetrator of the blow and that he might have fled to Ciutat Badia through the tunnel under the highway or hid there, two mossos agents went to check. It wasn't hard for them to find the suspect wrapped in a big blanket, sitting in front of the shack he used as shelter, immersed in filth. He spat at them and hurled insults. Not content with this salutation, he rose, unzipped his fly and aimed his piss at the policeman in front of him who leapt back and with a grimace of disgust reached mechanically for his weapon. He knew he was not supposed to fire; the law forbade shooting other than in self-defense. Neither could he descend to the level of the attacker and get into a pissing battle with him. He limited himself to raising his club and approached the vagrant menacingly. Then, as the *mosso* showed him his handcuffs from a distance, lest the poor devil hadn't finished emptying his bladder, the man produced a rock from his pocket with extraordinary swiftness and aimed it at the policeman's head, giving him a good bump. Then he bolted, taking advantage of the seconds his surprise attack had given him that had left the policeman in pain, but instead of heading for Ciutat Badia, ran uphill toward the Bellaterra campus and the spot where they had found Laura Cremona's body, a place still cordoned off. He stopped a few paces before the do-not-pass tape and with the agility of a cat, climbed the trunk of a pine tree and sat on a high branch. From that perch, rock in hand, he started to yell: "Sons of bitches, dirty assassins, do you know what you are doing? Do you know who I am? I am the Prince of Aquitaine, the owner of El Corte Inglés in Sabadell and I think also in Diagonal in the Barcelonas, the vice-president of the Barça Football Club. Did you know that? I enjoy parliamentary immunity, yes, me, and you cannot arrest me or attack me. Did you know that?"

Up there, he cut an even sorrier figure. He had lost the disgusting blanket-cape as he sprinted, a piece of fabric the color of infinite squalor. Being of a strong build and of an indefinite age, nearer forty than fifty to judge by his spryness, he was tall and athletic. Only his crazed eyes gave away his delusion. The rest of his features, rather harmonious and well proportioned, seemed like those of a sane person.

Two members of the forensic department, who had continued to gather samples and were the closest to the tree, approached the crazy man who, seeing them, showed them his rock with a triumphal burst of mirth and again took to yelling: "I am attacking in self-defense! I have a right to a home. A constitutionally guaranteed right. The Constitution says so: we are all entitled to a dignified existence. Yes, siree, if thieves come into my bathroom as I am relieving myself, I must defend my person. And if they threaten to cut my dick off, I must tell them, hey, not this, no way. Then I pick up a rock and hit them on the head. If I see a whore, what do I do? Only what decency dictates: Out, out! What did you think?"

The guys from the forensic department looked at each other, not knowing where to begin. There was no doubt the guy was deranged and aggressive and ought to be arrested. It also seemed quite clear that he was the perpetrator of the attack on Rosario Hurtado and might even be implicated in the death of Laura Cremona. They soon learned he had also hit one of their colleagues who was at the time being taken to the hospital.

21

The detention of Bartomeu Valldonzella i Artigues added a surreal and surprising twist to the case of Laura Cremona's murder. In other circumstances, finding that fool who claimed to be the Prince of Aquitaine, the Catalan son of the Spanish king, the owner of El Corte Inglésor, the president or vice-president of the Barça – his professed role within the football club varied according to Valldonzella's whim – would have been taken as one of the many grotesque episodes the mossos endured when encountering weirdos and crazy people. But the fact that he was found near the spot where Laura's body lay and that he attacked two police officers, forced the authorities to take opportune measures.

Since the mossos had strict orders to employ force only if necessary, it was very hard for them to talk the man into dropping his "weapon" as he called the rock he used to threaten them and get down from the tree. He refused at first and then said he would come down if someone climbed up to get him. A corporal who happened to be a rock-climbing enthusiast volunteered to do it. But seeing him start to get up the trunk, Valldonzella decided against the move: "Do you parasites think that you must send a monkey to fetch me? Shouldn't you be opening the door for me, the son of the King? I demand to come down by the stairs or by elevator. Come on, if you want me to drop the weapon and tell you about what I've seen in my comings and goings through these shitty woods, I'm here, waiting. Come on already!"

Aware that this bizarre situation was throwing a ridiculous light on the police and that if the press caught a wind of it they would have a feast day, the mossos decided to call Sabadell for reinforcements and close all access to the woods, both from campus and from the pathway to Ciutat Badia.

The reinforcements did not take long to arrive and brought along two firemen with a ladder. When he saw the ladder, Valldonzella shouted a couple of "bravos" and was happy to surrender. He came down waving to right and left like a prince at his subjects. He let them put handcuffs on him and was led peacefully, without another word to one of the cars the police had in the Letters parking lot from where he was taken to the Sabadell station which was now to be the main hub of the investigation.

The police were aware that Bartomeu Valldonzella i Artigues's testimony wouldn't help much, that he was unstable and suffered from some mental ailment. Still, they were most keen if there was no file on him, to take his fingerprints and see if they matched some of those found on Laura's body. They would then wait for the results of the autopsy to determine if there was a connection or if just a peculiar fortuity had brought together Bartomeu the madman and Laura the unfortunate.

The police discovered that Valldonzella, born in Lleida in 1970, a member of a well-to-do family and a lawyer by training, was suffering from severe schizophrenia that rendered him homeless and made him lead a tramp's existence, yet he had no police record. At the same time, at the Hospital Clínic's Forensic Anatomical Institute, Laura's cadaver, after being identified by her mothers, was under minute examination by the resident clinician and his team.

The Italian consul, who had walked Signore Cremona-Hogarth to the lobby of the Hospital Clínic, where their daughter's body was waiting, and who had promised them all help he could muster to facilitate transferring the remains to Milan as speedily as possible, stayed behind to speak with the examiner. It turned out he knew Doctor Golorons; they both attended a cigar club that met on Thursday evenings at the

Dry Martini. If Dante Braccalente could access directly the examiner's report, it would not be necessary to wait for the police to release the results of the autopsy to share with Signore Cremona-Hogarth who, exhausted and disconsolate, wished for nothing more than to move out of the Bellaterra hotel and leave Barcelona with Laura's remains to bury her in the family's plot in Milan.

The Italian consul thought himself fortunate, despite all the sad events, because he knew Golorons. This doctor had a good professional reputation for wielding the scalpel without first resorting to a shot of whiskey, unlike, he himself confided, he'd seen some colleagues do. One day he'd been invited to the consul's home and had mentioned to Dante that he was used to the sight of the effects of death on bodies and took it as one more component of his workday. As he knew all too well that the taboo against death had replaced the taboo against sex to a great extent in Western society, he avoided mentioning his medical specialization. He suspected that many imbeciles would look at him with disgust and shun him. He himself, however, found his work fascinating. To learn the causes of death was not only enriching but also supplied data that could help future generations. When he was told that Dante Braccalente wanted to see him, he asked for the consul to be shown in. He knew he could not break his vows of confidentiality, but understood how much the representative of Italy needed to know what conclusions he had reached and how long it would take for him to release the body.

22

The Italian consul, having sworn to absolute discretion, learned directly from the examiner that Laura Cremona had died of asphyxia in the early hours of her disappearance, between four and five o' clock in the morning on Saturday, 29th November. The killer or killers had strangled her using a scarf and once dead – there was no blood on the body – her vagina was slit in order to insert a plastic mouse into it, the sort of toy that novelty stores sold for jokes.

Doctor Golorons confessed to his friend, the consul, that he would have never imagined finding such an object inside a body. In all the autopsies he had carried out during a career stretching over twenty years, he had found, as he examined the rectums and vaginas, a strange element only three times – they had all been capsules with drugs. One would have to find out if the plastic mouse did or did not contain some narcotic substance that might relate Laura's death to drug trafficking, but that task fell to the police, not to him. He could only certify that neither the strangulation nor the incision had been carried out at the spot the cadaver had been found. The killer had put her clothes back on the body and it had been transported after death. There was no indication that the girl had struggled to defend herself. The body presented no blows or scratches and did not show bits of another person's skin under her nails. Traces of lorazepam detected in her stomach suggested they had wanted to anesthetize her before strangling her. If that were the case, she wouldn't have suffered.

Doctor Golorons had left the morgue for a moment to speak with Dante Braccalente who would rather not see the dead Laura. He preferred to remember her as she appeared in the photographs he had seen and was thankful to the doctor for the information.

"It looks like they attacked her from behind by surprise," said the doctor. "The imprint of the scarf's knot appears on the back of her neck; it must have been someone she knew and trusted. Or perhaps she had been lured to a sexual practice that is more prevalent among males: asphyxiation to intensify the orgasm. The traces of medication, however, do not support this."

"Was she raped?" Braccalente asked, supposing that the profanation of the body might have been accompanied by another humiliation.

"It doesn't look like it, although the analyses are not yet complete. Biological samples are still being examined. If she engaged in copulation before she died with her killer or another person, I suspect it was consensual. What I can tell you for sure is that the cut to her vagina was made after her death with a well-honed razor or a box cutter or some such instrument, with the intention of inserting the mouse. What was the objective? I do not know. I would assume revenge. The murderer must have had a relationship with the victim, but until he is caught and confesses, we will not know the significance of the plastic toy. Is it a part of a secret code between lovers? Who knows?"

"There is a young man in custody, the last person to see Laura alive," the consul said. "It looks like he has no alibi. If he turns out to be the murderer and is judged and condemned, then Signora Cremona might feel some consolation. It is always helpful to know that justice has been served." Then he asked if the examiner thought whether it might have been a rat that had gnawed off the piece of ear missing from the body.

"There is no missing bit. It looks that way because her right ear lobe was mangled by a door; I would surmise the trunk of the car that moved the body. The folks from the forensic department have gathered plenty of samples and they must be analyzing them now. If they point at the suspect, then the case will be easily resolved; otherwise, the matter is complicated. What I can tell you is that the mouse should provide some clue. If I were the police, I would give it my full attention."

"When do you think we can have the body? Laura's mother," Braccalente avoided using the plural to save himself the explanation for the moment, "would like to take it to Italy as soon as possible. I have promised her I would take care of the bureaucracy."

"On my part, I hope to finish today. I suppose you'll be able to have it tomorrow, but it's a Saturday...I do not know if the permissions office is open on Saturdays. Besides, tomorrow is a holiday. I am unfamiliar with repatriations, you surely know better than anyone. And now, if you'll excuse me, I've got to get back to work."

Doctor Golorons had received Dante Braccalente in the small office he probably used to write his reports. Because these documents, very technical, precise and full of clinical terms, could show little gaiety, the place also looked sad. The furniture itself seemed to mourn. The desk with the computer sat on twisted legs, just as the columns supporting two bookcases full of medical texts. Fortunately, the chairs on which they sat during their conversation were functional office pieces, quite neutral, as was a large filing cabinet. These must have been the only pieces of furniture to be renewed in about a century and a half. It had been decided, understandably, to abandon these offices and autopsy labs as soon as the ones in the new Justice building would be ready.

The consul, as he came out of the Forensic Anatomical Institute, ran to the nearest bar and ordered a whiskey with lots of ice. He sipped it, enjoying the liquor while he reviewed what the doctor had told him and he had sworn not to reveal. This excused him from having to explain to Signore Cremona-Hogarth that their daughter's body had been defiled. He figured that the murderer had not been satisfied by just killing Laura and wanted to further humiliate her. But what was the meaning of the plastic mouse?

When he left the bar, instead of rushing to see Laura's mothers as he had planned, he decided to go to the consulate. A most disagreeable weekend awaited him. He would also have to tell Andrea – whom he often called "my little rat or mouse,", terms he would never again use – that he wouldn't be able to take her out for a drive as he had promised last Monday, the last time they saw each other.

23

Both Dolors Adrover and Rosa Casasaies wore black when they went to see Signore Cremona-Hogarth on Saturday evening. They chose black not because they thought a mourning formality was called for, but rather because the hue reflected their downcast mood. The dean had resorted to tranquilizers and appeared calm. The adviser to the Erasmus scholars, by contrast, could barely control her whimpering as she rode the elevator to the third floor of the Hotel Claris in Barcelona, where Laura's mothers had moved the day before from their hotel in Bellaterra.

Joining them for their visit, the rector did not don a black necktie or any tie, but a gray turtleneck, and the Defender of the Students wore a high-quality black tie. Signore Cremona-Hogarth, wearing light-colored pants and sweaters, crushed by sorrow, seemed on the verge of drowning in even more disconsolate depths. Clara had dark circles under her eyes, an indication that she hadn't slept all night and Margaret seemed to have suddenly aged ten years; the lines on her forehead and her crow's feet, barely noticeable before, had become little furrows, as if the hands of a clock, frozen until then on her skin, had decided to make up for lost time and reveal the terrible truth of the years.

Even though both women were accustomed to social life, used to accepting the many nuisances of human relations with patience and good manners, they didn't bother to tolerate the visit any longer than ten minutes. It was them and not the rector who attended to the visitors, thanking them for their condolences in a cold manner and once again insisting that the university ought to pressure the police to release Laura's body so it could be taken back to Italy and buried in Milan as soon as possible. This was their sole interest. The memorial which would take place at the School of Letters on Tuesday in honor of their daughter did not seem to interest them. They didn't even ask what form it would have and who would take part in it.

Leaving the suite, now occupied by Signore Cremona-Hogarth, the rector remarked to his professors that he had the impression Laura's mothers blamed the university for what had happened to their daughter, which he thought most unfair. At the Autònoma everyone had treated her kindly. They could not harbor a grudge against any of them. But Rosa Casasaies's response made the rector realize that, given the circumstances they were enduring, it was normal for the Italian ladies to blame them. Laura had lived on campus, and even though the land where her body had been found did not belong to the university – a detail which the academic authorities wanted to make very clear – it was so close to the School of Letters that it was difficult to consider it alien to the campus. She, Rosa Casasaies, would probably have the same reaction if such a thing befell her daughter. Saying this, she felt a shiver and remembered the argument with Cristina she had that very afternoon about the time the girl said she wanted to come home Saturday night, between three and four o' clock in the morning. Her daughter didn't think twice about walking all by herself on the deserted streets of Barcelona. However empty the streets in the Gràcia neighborhood where they lived were, she insisted she was not afraid, that nothing bad would happen to her, that her parents' warnings masked a desire to control her. And when her mother reminded her that the Erasmus student had been found dead at the Autònoma, Cristina, with a naiveté that set Rosa's teeth on edge, retorted that it had happened in Bellaterra, not in Barcelona.

That very evening, Signore Cremona-Hogarth received another visitor. Thanks to the good offices of the Italian consul,

Josep Lluçanès, head of the criminal investigation unit of the Sabadell police, who was now in charge of the case, agreed not to ask them to come to his office and paid them a visit at the hotel. Sub-Inspector Manuela Vázquez, whom he had asked to cooperate in the investigation, accompanied Inspector Lluçanès. At this juncture, her presence would be useful to him. He hadn't met the ladies and, besides, he imagined that they, like most people, did not easily warm up to any sort of policeman. For this reason, perhaps because of their sexual orientation, they would prefer, as the lesser evil, a policewoman. He said so to Vázquez with a faint ironic smile, as they walked through the lobby of the Hotel Claris. Lluçanès had few dealings with Vázquez in the past, but he quickly sensed that what he had just said would seem out of line to her. Manuela smiled as she said: "I imagine they don't care about the sex of the police. I do not think their sexual orientation has anything to do with it. What they want is for us to be efficient and since we haven't been able to find Laura alive, we should at least release her body."

When they approached the reception desk, the receptionist took them for a foreign couple and asked in English whether they had a reservation. With a stern look, the head of the criminal investigation unit told the receptionist that he was wrong and to please contact room 310. From his very serious tone of voice, Manuela Vázquez thought he'd felt offended. The inspector was tall, quite handsome, with an air of superiority and sure of himself. A definitely attractive type. Manuela herself usually went unnoticed, a sign that her features had little distinction. She did not linger longer than necessary before the mirror, pausing just to run a comb through her hair, perhaps because the image she saw in it wasn't gratifying: round face, potato nose, myopic eyes, not tall, short legs and plump. But this did not bother her in the least. Even though her looks never worried her, not even when she was young, she noticed at once that Lluçanès found her physique dismissible, which might have been the reason he had felt offended by the receptionist who could not see that she did not suit him as a mate, that he needed to be next to a woman with more class and that she could not possibly be his spouse, but rather his secretary or a subordinate.

The Italian consul was waiting for them in the suite's sitting room and the meeting went on for a little longer than the one with the academic authorities. Both the inspector and the sub-inspector felt uncomfortable which made them sit upright on the couch. They had racked their brains for the least disagreeable terms in which to answer the questions they expected to be posed about the autopsy. The mothers had every right to know all the details, but some, such as the degradation of the body and the insertion of the plastic mouse, were hard to swallow. The sub-inspector thought it best to postpone the examination of the details until they could explain what significance those might have had for the murderer. On the other hand, the inspector believed they ought to know. Perhaps the women could find some connection to some aspect of their daughter's friendships. But the mothers did not ask any questions, not even what, in such cases, family members always wanted to know: whether the girl had been raped. They probably avoided asking about this in order not to add to the pain of hearing obscene references to what they already felt. In the end, the inspector decided not to bring it up either.

24

During the twenty-minute interview, the only thing Clara Cremona asked the police was the time when the mothers would be able to claim Laura's body. As soon as the inspector told her that they could have it on Monday, both Clara and Margaret shut themselves into an obstinate and hostile silence. It seemed like that the piece of information was all they needed and that they were indifferent to anything else they might be told.

Clara seemed absent-minded; she had a blank stare and an ashy veil dulled her eyes. She occasionally petted the teddy bear she had been carrying around since Laura's disappearance. Next to her, Margaret was continuously smoking, lighting a cigarette with the butt of another, intent only on filling her lungs with tar.

It appeared as though they didn't care about what Lluçanès was telling them: the freeing of Marcel Bru after it had been ascertained from the examiner's report that Laura's death had occurred between four and five o'clock in the morning, a time he had been with his friends as they declared. Since his alibi was valid, as the judge had deemed, there was no reason to keep him in jail.

Nor did the women show any interest when the inspector told them the investigation would be taking a different route if Bru's guilt was dismissed and the arrested Valldonzella was implicated. The fact that this man was mentally ill did not mean he was unable to have killed Laura or to have attacked her after Bru dropped her off. But they needed proof it had been

Valldonzella and they still had none. There were other open lines. They were inquiring about the guests at the campus hotel on the night the young woman was killed. They were also investigating some drifters who had made their home in an abandoned villa near Bellaterra. The following Monday, the police would go back to cross-examining the students and professors who had any dealings with the dead girl and the vanished Erasmus student. As for him, since the day before, they had some leads: the junk folder of Laura's e-mail showed a message from Iliescu. Iliescu had sent it at mid-morning on the day he was to move to Bellaterra. It informed her that he was delaying his decision to move in with her and Domenica; he wanted to think it over and might take advantage of those days with canceled classes to travel to Romania. That undelivered e-mail threw some light on his mysterious disappearance. Iliescu could be in some part of his country undetected by the Romanian police. His disappearance had to be considered separately from Cremona's case, even though indirectly, by an accumulation of senseless coincidences, it was its cause. If the guy had not vanished, Laura would not have denounced his disappearance and Bru would not have accompanied her that night and she would not have run into her murderer, whoever he was.

Back in Sabadell, where Lluçanès was to meet his team and Manuela Vázquez was to drop by the hospital where Rosario Hurtado was still admitted, the inspector told Vázquez that he often had to break such terrible news to relatives and friends of victims throughout his long career and had become used to their reactions, which went from tears and wails to fainting or even catatonic stupors. But the cold silence with which Signore Cremona-Hogarth had received his words seemed to him of a different nature altogether.

"The fact that they didn't ask a thing," he said, "that they showed no interest whatsoever in the investigation makes me suppose that they do not trust us one bit. They might still consider us, like many foreigners do, a Third World country, with an ineffective, corrupt and undemocratic police force, and this really gets my goat. Things have changed a lot since Franco's death; we are now a member of the European Union, but the old clichés still rule: *Spain is different* which includes us, Catalans. I would not have suspected this of them, such sophisticated, knowledgeable and elegant ladies, as you told me they were."

"Do you have children?" Manuela Vázquez asked Josep Lluçanès instead of responding to what he'd just said.

"Yeah, two: a nine-year-old girl and a six-year-old boy. And you?"

"A twenty-year-old adolescent girl; you know that adolescence nowadays lasts till thirty…If what has happened to Laura had happened to my daughter, I think I'd throw myself out the first high window. I wouldn't be able to bear it. I understand the ladies' apathy, I get that nothing interests them. Even if we find the murderer, it won't make Laura come back to life."

As soon as she said this, she thought she should have kept quiet, that perhaps Lluçanès would take that hypothetical "throw myself out a high window" as a sign of mental instability, too emotional for a police officer.

"Now that I think of it, my wife would also react like you if something like this happened to Caterina. Not me, I would not stop until I had found the culprit and made him pay, I assure you."

"We are conditioned by biology," the sub-inspector added, just to say something. "Even when facing the same stimuli, men and women have different reactions."

"The consul didn't open his mouth either," Lluçanès recalled, as though by stating the fact, he contradicted Manuela's somewhat pedantic sentiment.

"I think his silence has been out of respect for them, out of discretion," the sub-inspector explained. 'He is an affable guy and has lived in Barcelona a long time, he is not given to commonplace talk; I am sure he respects us. He has given ample proof these last few days that he's ready to cooperate. No matter how disturbed he might be, he does not belong to

Laura's family; he hadn't even met her and cannot be affected as much as her mothers."

Before Manuela Vázquez got out of the car at the corner of the Sabadell hospital, Josep Lluçanès asked her if the following day, a Sunday, she'd be available for duty. When she said yes, that he could count on her, he informed her he had called a meeting of his team and wanted her to attend with her closest associates, because he thought that together they would have an easier time finishing the task as quickly as possible, which was the arrest of the perpetrator or perpetrators.

25

The campus security patrol was the first to be alerted that the door to apartment number 2 on the third floor of the university's Vila A showed signs of forced entry. A neighbor from the same floor called them. He was a veterinary student who noticed that its door was ajar. Like every morning, whether a workday or a holiday, that Sunday, at seven, he had left his apartment, two doors down, to go to the pool for his usual swim. He also told them that he believed there was no one inside because he could hear nothing and that he hadn't gone in.

The patrol took but five minutes to show up, get to the third floor and the apartment. Thinking the place was empty, as the student had told them it appeared to be, Albert Rodés and Claudio Rodríguez stepped in to see if there was any other damage apart from the broken lock that would show that whoever had forced his way in hadn't done so because he'd lost his key, but rather because he wasn't meant to get in. Their first supposition was that someone wanted to steal electronic gadgets. Not long ago, a gang had raided the computer cluster in the School of Communications and had cleaned it out. From then on, a number of petty thieves had pestered the campus with smaller-scale thefts. Up to that point, it seemed as if the burglars were happy with a loot of laptop computers, cell phones, iPhones and iPods that students and professors carried in their backpacks or briefcases. All it took was a second's distraction to make the devices fade away as if by magic. The thieves might have gotten a little more brazen now. From classrooms and libraries, they had graduated to breaking into apartments. If this were not an isolated case, they would have to increase vigilance. But as far as they could see once inside, whoever had entered that apartment was not interested in electronics; there was an open laptop on a desk in the living room and a cell phone and an iPod on the couch.

"The person or persons who have forced open the lock to the apartment in the campus Vila did not do so to steal," Àngel Carmona, the Autònoma's head of security said with an edgy voice to the agent on duty at the Cerdanyola station when he answered the call. "Their motive was worse." Carmona might have thought that if he didn't say the word out loud, if he didn't say "to kill," there might be time to save the victim.

"Your people must come right away," he added. "We've already called the hospital for an ambulance."

It was on Sunday, 7th December at 8:23 a.m. that Carmona called the sub-inspector from her office.

Manuela Vázquez was supposed to be off-duty that day, a well-earned respite after a hectic week, but because Lluçanès had asked her to continue on Laura Cremona's case, she had gone early to her office. She wanted to have another look at the notebook where she had been writing facts and her impressions on the case. She also wanted a change of venue to calmly mull over the developments of the last few hours – the discovery of Laura's body, the arrest of Valldonzella and the release of Bru. Her own home did not allow her any peace and quiet, as the place had been invaded by her daughter's friends celebrating one of their birthdays by playing music and laughing loud enough to keep her awake most of the night.

She wanted time to decide whether the fool who had attacked the mossos had anything to do with Laura's death or not, but the phone call wrecked her plans. Talking to her, Àngel Carmona was more specific to reveal that there had been a victim, a young woman. She'd been found in her bed by two security guards at the Vila and showed signs of having been strangled.

The sub-inspector listened to the shaken voice of the head of security: 'I can't understand how such a thing could have happened. We have stepped up vigilance since Cremona's body was found; I can assure you that my men haven't had a moment's rest, after what they've been thorough. This morning at seven, just before the change of shifts, they told me all was quiet and there hadn't been any incident...'

Without hanging up, Manuela dialed agent Rifà's number on her cell and pressed an emergency code. As soon as Rifà answered, she ordered him to contact immediately the patrol closest to the campus and send them to the Vila without wasting a second and also inform the Sabadell forensic department and find Inspector Lluçanès. Manuela Vázquez had managed to develop the capability of doing two things at once without losing concentration, as if to disprove some psychological tenets. After talking to Rifà and still listening to Carmona, she stopped short his excuses about the good job his subordinates did and asked him if they knew who the dead woman was. The head of security hadn't yet found out the victim's name. All he could say was that she was young, blonde, tall, probably an Erasmus scholar and the place where she'd been found was apartment number 2 on the third floor of the Vila's A building. Since there was no one in the Vila's administrative office during weekends, they'd been unable to find out whom the apartment had been leased to. One of his men had looked for some document to identify the young woman in a bag hanging from a chair in the living room. But Rodríguez was a substitute and it seemed like he didn't know that in such circumstances one should not touch anything and that one should wait for the police. Carmona apologized for Rodríguez's behavior. He couldn't understand how that had happened, it made no sense to him, as if some powerful being had set a voodoo curse on them, as if the students, the 4,000 professors and the 3,000 instructors had all, one by one, stepped into shit.

The sub-inspector recalled that she had already heard such sentiments. In her opinion, what had happened had nothing to do with a supernatural power, but was the result of a wicked fate, a conjunction of chance events that had brought about a tragedy. But she allowed the head of security to go on as she pulled her notebook from a drawer and placed it in her coat's pocket. She went to the window and saw that luckily it wasn't raining and ended the conversation, telling Carmona that she was on her way to the Vila and would be there in less than ten minutes.

After hanging up, she sat for a second, swallowed hard and rubbed her eyes with her fists to avert tears. She had no doubt that the dead woman was Domenica Arrigo. She felt sorry for Domenica. It was a waste of another young life and provoked a dark rage in her. Besides, she was mad at herself and wondered if she could have avoided it by asking her superiors for protection for Domenica.

26

When she saw Domenica Arrigo's body, Manuela Vázquez again had to make an effort to stem the flow of tears. She did not want to appear overly emotional to her colleagues; nor did she want them to interpret her crying as female weakness. Even though her scar might never go away, Manuela envied Rosario Hurtado for not having to face such bitter news. The blow from the rock prevented the agent from discovering how unhinged people could get and the degree of murderous instinct they could nurse without anyone noticing it.

She was thinking that surely the anomaly that prevented psychopaths from respecting a person's life lay in their deranged minds. But until scientific advances found the specific medicine to treat them, society would continue under threat. This is why stricter protective measures were called for and why now she had to use all her five senses to find the perpetrator. When she got to the apartment, the people from the forensic department had already placed a floodlight and tripods in the room to take pictures. They roamed about in their white coveralls, which lent them a certain weightless air. They were dusting for fingerprints and any indication that would give them a clue about the murderer before the examiner and the judge ordered the body's removal.

The sub-inspector mused that one did not need to be particularly sharp or observant to assume a link between the deaths of Laura and Domenica. The murderer or murderers had followed the same method. The only difference was that instead of a muffler, it was now a white scarf tied around the victim's neck. Domenica lay on her back, her hair mussed up with some tresses over her face, her body covered by a blanket except for her right shoulder and arm. Her mouth was open, her face stiff and showing a bloody hue around her eyelids. Her eyes were wide open, their corneas misty and the orbs softened, her tongue hanging out. Her face was a scary sight and looked nothing like that of the living Domenica, which had been pleasant and jolly. Her murderer must have really hated her, Manuela thought and she remembered Bru who had been walking free since Friday afternoon.

Feeling sick, she walked out to the landing where a technician was examining the lock and taking fingerprints from the forced door. She needed to telephone Dante Braccalente who was having terrible luck: Domenica was also an Italian, her death would also fall on his docket as he would have to call her family and inform Signore Cremona-Hogarth who, with Domenica's help, had gathered Laura's belongings on Friday evening. Now they would have to be pestered again with unpleasant questions. But the consul did not answer and Manuela had to leave a message asking him to get in touch with her as quickly as possible.

Manuela Vázquez could not get poor Domenica out of her head. She had seen how devastated she was on Friday, yet Vázquez hadn't thought of advising her to move out of the apartment. Campus surveillance had intensified. No one had suspected that Laura's tragedy would have a second act. She needed to know Domenica's moves during the hours preceding her death, where she'd been and with whom she'd spoken. Had she met Bru? The sub-inspector recalled that when she entered the apartment, she had seen the girl's cell phone and laptop on the sofa. By now, the gloved hands of the people from the forensic department must have already picked those up and that very morning they would check calls and e-mails. This convinced her that she ought to prepone the meeting with Professor Bellpuig that she had scheduled for the following Tuesday and looked into her notebook for the professor's home phone number in case he had already returned to Barcelona. When he answered, without mentioning that Domenica was dead, she requested to see him in her Cerdanyola office that very afternoon, apologized for calling him on a Sunday and told him that exchanging views on some of his Erasmus students had become as imperative as it was urgent. Bellpuig seemed to agree gladly. He had one request only: to be told how he could get to the station using public transportation.

"I'm a good citizen, concerned about the planet's sustainability," he added wryly. "I always try to use the metro, the train or the bus."

She had just hung up when Lluçanès, whom she'd seen arrive a few seconds before, came back out to the landing to get her. He wanted her to observe a detail in the corpse: bits of black plastic sticking out from under the victim's tongue.

The inspector recalled that in some ancient Greek rituals, they stuck a coin under a dead person's tongue as payment for Charon the ferryman, and perhaps the murderer had wanted a variation on the practice. But until the examiner got there, they could not touch the body. Everything was ready for his arrival: the body bag and plastic protectors for the victim's hands in case she had marks on them if she had fought for her life.

Robert Amorós, the judge, had certified many deaths in the course of his long career, and so death had stopped affecting him, except in cases of young people. As he saw it, folks who had died in accidents or as was the case with the murdered girl, who had their lives taken before their time, had died out of turn. He often both signed the order to take the body to the examiner's office and as a kind of afterword, ranted against the madness of mankind, the only mammals, he said, capable of killing without motive or of provoking accidents by their dead-set stubbornness to follow traffic rules. This time, having arrived before the examiner, as he waited for the clinician, he reversed his procedure and with a potent and enraged voice that fit the occasion, cursed the fiend who had brought about that tragedy. Five minutes later, he was still cursing the "degenerate monster" capable of such a deed when the examiner came in, a thin and tall man, very young, a figure that contrasted with the judge's chubby and old one.

"I am Jordi Pujol, but you can see I am not the great politician," he introduced himself, emphasizing the adjective "great." He confessed he had just gotten the job and was quite new in that line of work. As he noticed a certain wariness in the eyes of both the judge and the inspector, he added he'd been trained by Doctor Golorons himself from whom he had learned much. Lluçanès would have preferred the latter and not Pujol to take care of the autopsy. Besides being well-known and respected in his profession, Golorons had overseen the examination of Laura's body, which would have allowed him to reach more precise conclusions about the murderer's motives.

As soon as the examiner was ready, the inspector asked him to find out what had been placed under Domenica's tongue. Pujol, before reaching in with gloved fingers, said: "It was used for speaking and for kissing, and now …" He extracted a black plastic cockroach such as those children and even grown-ups use for pranks.

"God," the judge said, "what kind of sick fuck …"

"It might be a reference to the ancient Egyptian scarab, a symbol of the constant transformation of existence," the forensic examiner mused as he dropped the cockroach into a bag. "We must be facing a ritual murderer. I've read somewhere that the Egyptians believed that if the dead had a scarab with them, they could come back to life." And with a supercilious smile, he added, looking at the policemen, "but I don't think this is the case for this poor kid."

Neither Lluçanès nor Vázquez made a comment. They were more interested in the time of death than in the symbolic interpretations the examiner offered. Both police officers asked for his opinion; first the sub-inspector and then the inspector who pressed on. Pujol did not want to rush to conclusions and said he could provide valid data only after a detailed examination of the unfortunate victim's viscera in the autopsy room of the Forensic Anatomical Institute. But Lluçanès insistence finally got the medical man to say that he believed Domenica had been dead for more than twelve hours, between twelve and twenty-four. As a justification he added: "*Rigor mortis* normally appears sometime between thirty minutes and three hours after death and then the cadaver begins to relax as you can observe with this poor girl."

Pujol hypothesized that Domenica had probably been attacked when she slept because it appeared she had not put up a fight. There were no signs of violence on her hands or arms, but this was a hurried supposition that would have to be re-examined in the lab after the autopsy.

27

Leaving the Vila apartment, which was now cordoned off by the police and still guarded by two agents, Manuela Vázquez walked to the campus hotel. She had half an hour before the 11 o'clock meeting Lluçanès had called for at the Egara Complex in Sabadell. She had a little time to drink a cup of coffee and write down the facts she considered useful in her notebook. She wrote without any specific plan, as things came to her mind, the way she did during her early years of marriage when she jotted down the grocery shopping lists for the holidays, Christmas presents for her husband, in-laws and siblings all jumbled together. She first wrote that early on Tuesday, she should send someone to the novelty stores in Barcelona and the Vallès area; the Internet sales of plastic objects for jokes should also be investigated so as to cast a line in that direction. She added: "The mouse and the cockroach are macabre signs left purposely by a serial murderer intent on killing young women. He might have even "Googled" references to technique, following strict guidelines. Go over the Web sites. But neither the deck-of-cards murderer nor the Putxet assassin showed quite this symmetry. We face a perfectionist and a clever psychopath here, which makes me think it isn't Bru, though I could be wrong. We must interrogate him again and, before that, find out the exact time when the judge released him. The murderer belongs to the young women's circle. He is not a total stranger, he knew them well. The forced lock might be a ruse; Domenica could have opened the door because she knew him well and then he mangled the lock to create a false lead. We must investigate Professor Bellpuig. Check the guest list at the hotel. Try to find out more about the occupying crowd. Not all are students. Study the files we have on protestors. Get the list of the campus security employees; they also patrol at night."

Finally she ended her notes: "The murderer is an old guy who hates youth. Hates beauty. He is ugly, old. Is he a professor? A security guard?"

Then, in all caps, she wrote: "BUT WE MUST WAIT FOR DOMENICA'S AUTOPSY."

As soon as she had written this last phrase, her cell phone rang and she answered it, thinking it might be the Italian consul. The person calling her was crying and from the sobs, even before a word was said, one could tell it was a woman. The rector himself had alerted Rosa Casasaies. She was crushed, wretched and kept asking Manuela what Manuela had been asking herself: "Why? But why? Can you tell me?" And she added: "Catch him, Manuela, catch him and make him pay. He should pay with two death sentences for what he has done."

Casasaies's call delayed Manuela and she arrived five minutes late for the meeting, just at the moment when Mateu Samper, the director-general of the Interior ministry came in, perfectly shaved and with an impeccable tie. He was there "simply to show up, given the importance of these horrible events," he said, "even though I must go back to Barcelona right away." Before leaving, however, he managed to get in a little speech. He seldom had the chance to speak, a sad state of affairs because he thought himself a man with a gift for oratory greater than that of the whole cabinet put together. He told the police officers that it was imperative to solve the case promptly, that the good name of the mossos was at stake, not to mention the prestige of the Bellaterra campus and even that of Catalonia. He insisted that the university should return to business as usual by all means, that he had given his promise that very morning to the rector and to the superintendent of universities, who were, as he spoke, still in a meeting with the minister of the interior and the Italian consul. Then he inquired, confidentially to be sure, if they had any leads and also insisted that both directors, but primarily the superintendent of universities, were in agreement that news should be most prudently revealed to the press. The less talk there was about this, the better, and the mossos could do their job more smoothly.

Lluçanès looked affectionately at his team and introduced each one by name to this nattily-dressed authority who had risen to that post thanks to years of warming up a seat in the party office. He assured the man that every one of them, beginning with himself, were committed to working full time on the Cremona-Arrigo case, that they would not rest until they found the perpetrator of the crimes. Lluçanès took advantage of the moment to request reinforcements. As for leads, since they were so sparse, he preferred to focus on the moral portrait of the murderer.

"We are facing a meticulous and smart psychopath," he said, "who plans his actions carefully as I see it, which makes him more dangerous. Besides killing young women, which might signify problems relating to the female sex or some childhood trauma with his mother, he is also alienated from the university community. We must look for him among those people who might have felt hurt or offended lately. Some professor who did not pass the certification exams, an instructor who did not get a fellowship or an expelled student."

"Hold it! Not a professor!" the director-general burst out. "A professor would not be a good idea." He was a man who at a certain period in his life alternated between chair-warming at the party's headquarters and taking classes at the School of Education on Tuesdays and Thursdays and he still felt most satisfied with his university degree.

"We hope it's not a professor," Lluçanès said with a touch of irony in his voice. "It would certainly be bad publicity and disastrous for the Autònoma. It might be someone in the administration or a student, but it's got to be someone who knows the campus, who is part of it. What do you think, sub-inspector?"

"I agree," replied Manuela. "Or it could be someone who is tied to the campus in some other way. The fact that both girls were Italian makes me think of the possibility that the murderer could be a member of the Italian community here; we will check if we have a file on any of them."

The director-general looked at his watch and got up. The others did the same. "Please, continue," he said, "don't get up. I have to go. The minister told me that in order to not create a general alarm, it would be best to delay contacting the press for as long as possible; let me insist on this. The government has no intention to disallow anything; that must be clear. But we will do a better job if the news doesn't spread. I know that the rectorate has ordered the press office not to contact the media until we have a reliable lead to arrest the criminal. I hope that the autopsy gives us such a lead." Then he shook hands with Lluçanès and said to him: "Keep me informed of any progress." Addressing the team, he uttered a generalized farewell: "Take it easy." But realizing the phrase wasn't precisely appropriate, he corrected himself: "Or rather, *don't*; in this case, I do think you must take it hard."

As soon as Mateu Samper left the meeting, the inspector, looking at the four people in front of him, asked if they had any questions. Bernat Lluc, the corporal in his team, a tall young fellow with a beaky face who was a fan of motorcycle racing, raised his hand.

"Shoot," the inspector said to Lluc.

"Are we discarding the possibility that it is a woman, sir?"

"No," Lluçanès replied. "We cannot discard any option until we find the criminal, man or woman. Sure, it could be a woman, although in the last forty years of criminal history, we've seen just two cases of women who have committed serial murders. Sub-inspector Vázquez can tell you better than I; she has a degree in psychology, besides being a good professional." He observed the effect of his praise on Manuela. "Such anomalous recurrence is much more frequent in the male psychopathology than in the female," he continued. "Whatever the sex, the Autònoma's murderer, let me insist, is someone who knows the campus well, who moves easily there and has his or her den nearby. I know we cannot search all the area's housing developments in depth, not even all the apartments in the Vila, but we can be on the lookout, especially at night. It's not unlikely that the murderer makes another move perhaps next week. I trust the forensic department can soon give us data to help, but in the meanwhile, I'm going to assign some jobs."

Looking to his right, where Corporal Lluc sat, he said to him: "Go to Hotel Serhs and obtain the list of guests who had a room there from Friday afternoon to Saturday this week and last. Check if there is a file on any of them. Talk to the receptionists. Get a list of all the employees. I remind you all that the hotel sits next to the Vila."

Then he looked at the rest of them and read some notes he produced from his pocket. Proceeding from Lluc, from right to left, he told agent Cañizares, an Andalusian, the son of a white father and a gypsy mother from Puerto de Santa María and probably the most colorful *mosso* in his jurisdiction, to question all the neighbors in building A of the Vila. He was to ask them if they knew the people who frequented the girls' apartment and if they had seen or heard anything out of the ordinary from Friday night on and if anyone had noticed the door being forced open. He insisted, furthermore, that Cañizares restrain from laughing because his laugh involved a kind of squeal that was contagious, even for detainees, a factor someone had once described as torture. He was to pay attention to whether or not the apartment had been broken into before Domenica was murdered, in which case, and since the examiner had put the time of death between twelve and twenty-four hours previous, how was it possible that nobody had noticed it before this morning? He was to interrogate neighbors on the same floor one by one and take notes of the hours when they had walked past the door.

Next to Cañizares was agent Llobera. Lluçanès didn't think he was the sharpest tool in the shed; when the rest of the team were on their way back, he was still taking his time. But despite his slowness in catching up, he was meticulous and often noticed details his comrades had missed. The inspector asked him to accompany Cañizares; he was sure there'd be work for the two of them. Then he addressed Manuela: "When will Rosario be discharged?"

"Today. She told me yesterday she wanted to get back to work as soon as possible.'"

"Then she should find Bru and ask him where he went and what he did once the judge released him last Friday afternoon."

"And what do you want me to do, Inspector?" Manuela asked.

"What you told me you'd do: go speak with Professor Bellpuig and if you think it advisable, ask Rifà to accompany Rosario and go to the Italian Consulate tomorrow to see if we can find any Italian nationals we have files on."

"If you agree, Inspector," said Manuela, "Rifà could also visit novelty stores in Barcelona and in the Vallès area, besides checking which outlets sell plastic mice and cockroaches online. They might recall some recent customers and could be a help."

"Very well. Call me when you're done with Bellpuig and if you don't mind a piece of advice, don't reveal to him at first that Domenica is dead. Let him talk."

28

Professor Bellpuig arrived on time for his appointment with the sub-inspector. He joked about her name as it was so close to that of his old friend, Manolo Vázquez.

"Are you as good a cook as he is?" he inquired. "Are you related?"

"Unfortunately, I am neither a relative nor a good cook. I like to answer in the affirmative when people ask me because I've read him. At home we have many of his Carvalho detective novels…"

She was going to say that the books were her ex-husband's, but didn't. Details of her failed marriage were none of Bellpuig's business. She opened with a trivial question: "You knew him? They say he was charming."

"Yes, I knew him well. We shared a prison cell for some months in Lleida, but charming, what you could call charming…He himself wrote that he was as charming as Aznar. But I suppose, Senora Vázquez, that you haven't called me here to talk about Manolo, but about the Cremona case," he added with a touch of irony. "I have no problem, quite the contrary, to cooperate with the new democratic police who are at the service of all." So as to display his willingness to cooperate, Bellpuig started by admitting that he had been a guest at the campus hotel before Manuela could mention that his name was on the lists of guests for the nights of Friday the 28th when Laura disappeared and Friday the 5th, when her body was found. A cool and collected Bellpuig explained his motives for staying at the Serhs, but begged the policewoman for discretion. Not because of himself (he was divorced and didn't have to respond to anyone), nor for the sake of his children (he didn't have any – that he knew of), but to protect the reputation of the person who had met him on those nights, his young lover. He explained that the day before yesterday, the night from Friday to Saturday, he hadn't planned to stay at the hotel. It was Mònica – "let me call her this for the moment," he said with a grin – who had requested meeting him there, insisting time and again, pestering him by phone the whole week he'd been away from Barcelona. Since he was a member of a promotions tribunal at Madrid's Complutense University which was to meet again on Monday, he had written to his dean, requesting leave to remain in Madrid. He wanted to use the rest of the days to continue his research on the Baroque *vanitates* in the Prado museum and in any case, there were no classes at the Autònoma because of the pickets.

"Do you know what I am talking about?" he asked with a superior air. As Manuela nodded, he went on. "To tell the truth, it suited me fine to be away from campus, from Mònica and from Domenica Arrigo."

The sub-inspector asked him to elaborate. Bellpuig alluded to a chance encounter with Domenica at the hotel bar where he was sipping a glass of whiskey, bored and annoyed because Mònica had just told him not to wait for her, that she couldn't spend the night with him because she hadn't been able to find a babysitter. The lonely drink was followed by one or two more. Then he ran into Domenica. He never expected to end in her bed just a couple of hours later in one of the Vila apartments. He was led there like a lamb by a rope, as his Mallorcan grandmother would have said, almost bewitched by the magnetism of that girl, thinking only of proving himself worthy of her attentions. In fact, he was so worried that he told her he could not promise exceptional service when she openly and unabashedly proposed making love.

He told her that he could not manage a *ménage à trios* and if Laura wasn't home, she could be in any moment from her television interview. No need to worry about that, Domenica informed him; they would not be bothered. She would hang the "DO NOT DISTURB" sign from her bedroom doorknob. The fact that Laura had just texted her saying she would not be late – implying that Domenica ought to think of some entertainment for the two of them – didn't matter to Domenica. The two girls had agreed on the significance of the sign.

It might have been the drinks, Bellpuig continued, that persuaded him to risk getting into an involvement that wasn't advisable. The Bellaterra campus was not, thank the gods, a North American campus, where going to bed with a student could cost even the most prestigious professor his job, but he was aware that many of his colleagues would disapprove. He didn't want to think what his dean's opinion would be if she learned about the tryst. But he would be a fool not to take advantage of the opportunity Domenica was offering him for free.

"You must think me a male chauvinist," he went on, "unable to accept that we've reached a moment in history when women can choose their sexual partners, which has only been a privilege of the males until now." Then he went on to say that what he had done with that student was simply a way to combat his boredom by assuaging the erotic tension of his still young hormones.

For a moment – he confided in Manuela Vázquez – he recalled the parties of his adolescence when he was stuck with the uglier girls, those the boys asked for a dance only when all the pretty girls had been taken. But it was only for a moment, because he immediately superimposed a more positive image on the negative one of his person. It was the image he tried to evoke when he taught a class, presented a lecture or was being interviewed to discuss his specialization – Baroque art. Yeah, the image of the self-assured intellectual, Manuela Vázquez was thinking, confident of his own ideas, aware that from this security flowed his most seductive weapon. It was a stereotype she knew well. His interlocutor's eyes made him rather seductive despite the hair-challenged orb of his head – a trait Manuela detested – and his puffy, sagging cheeks matching his double chin that gave him a slight resemblance to a turkey.

The sub-inspector had learned from Wikipedia that Bellpuig would turn fifty-five by the end of December, an age when his soul, according to Aristotle, would have been dead for five years. Despite this – he was now saying – his "latest victim" (referring to his lover and suggesting he might be exaggerating, for Mònica did not quite merit being termed "partner"), was very young, only four years older than Domenica. By going to bed with the Italian, he might have meant to pay back Mònica for making him stay at the Bellaterra hotel with the promise they could spend the night together and standing him up at the last minute.

This was why Mònica had to keep insisting for the whole of the past week for him to again book a room at the Bellaterra hotel and while he yielded, he didn't know if what he wanted was to see her again or rather enjoy another night with Domenica. He said that he spent the week thinking of Domenica and found it hard to concentrate on his work. He felt very satisfied when, Thursday afternoon, he received an e-mail from the student in which she said she needed to talk to him urgently. He replied he was not in Barcelona, but would be back on Saturday and if it was all right with her, they could meet for brunch; he could pick her up at her apartment at ten.

The sub-inspector's cell phone suddenly rang. She took the call and listened for no more than a couple of seconds. Hanging up, she looked at Bellpuig whom she had been listening to with concentration, noting down from time to time some aspect of his long monologue that she thought relevant and asking no questions. The tactic, designed to inspire confidence, usually worked well. The interrogated person, not suspecting anything, would fall into the trap they themselves had set with the strings of their own contradictions. Bellpuig, for the moment, had managed quite well, but he still had things to explain.

"My colleagues at the police forensic department," Manuela said at last, "just asked me for your fingerprints. If you don't mind, please follow me."

"Of course I don't mind," Bellpuig said. "I told you I have no problem cooperating with a democratic police…but can you tell me why you need my fingerprints?"

"Because you were at Domenica Arrigo's apartment, Professor Bellpuig, and poor Domenica, like her friend, has been murdered."

29

Manuela Vázquez returned to her office, carrying a tray with a cup of coffee and a water bottle. Professor Bellpuig was already waiting for her, standing by the window, and did not move when he heard her. The agent who had taken his fingerprints in an upstairs office had brought him back and told him he would inform the sub-inspector when they were done.

Manuela Vázquez was surprised when she saw Bellpuig facing out the window because it was dark outside and he could see nothing. As if guessing her puzzlement, he told her as he turned around that he felt a special attraction for looking outside; since he was a child, the first thing he did was look for a window whenever he entered a room, especially when he felt distressed as he did now. The news of Domenica's death had shaken him up.

He paused and picked up the coffee cup Vázquez offered and downed the coffee in exactly three gulps without sugar. Then he sat on the same chair he'd occupied before and even though Manuela Vázquez did not ask a question, he went on, softly, miserably:

"I learned about Laura's death from the TV news program last Friday night when I was in the Bellaterra hotel's room waiting for Mònica. I was horrified. I didn't even know she had disappeared. Bear in mind that I left last Sunday for Madrid, exactly one week ago and I immediately thought Domenica was in danger. Had it not been because Mònica was due to arrive soon, I would have gone to her apartment, even if that meant running into other kids who could also be my students and might be shocked to see me there. But then I calmed down, thinking that my idea would have occurred to the police also and there must have been some protection in place for Domenica."

He took a sip of water, pulled out a pack of cigarettes and lit one. Realizing he hadn't asked if it was OK to smoke, he gestured as if asking for indulgence for his impatience. Manuela Vázquez smiled and he offered her one. She shook her head. Smoking despondently, he went on:

"During the days I spent in Madrid, I put what was going on in Bellaterra out of my mind. I didn't even know if the police had made any progress in the search for Iliescu. The Madrid papers were the only ones I saw and I just skimmed through them; I read nothing in them about Laura's disappearance. Jaume Pocoví, my teaching assistant, said nothing to me either. He was to be my substitute in case the occupiers allowed a return to classes; I had asked him to go to the Autònoma every day, not just when he felt like it, as is his wont. Of course, you cannot trust him..."

"I see you do not get along," the sub-inspector interrupted.

'I can't stand him,' he admitted candidly. 'He lives in a world of his own. I have warned him I'll write a negative report. He is of no use to me and I don't want him next year. He might even have missed the second disappearance. Since his little friend dropped him, he's a changed man, interested in nothing. I think he's become autistic."

Manuela Vázquez thought the poor student served as Bellpuig's scapegoat and was made to suffer the professor's bad moods. She reflected the professor must be the type of person who was strong with the weak and weak with the strong. That would explain why while in an uncomfortable position, he presented himself as affable and even regaled her with a little excursus about people who disconnected from their surrounding reality and those who were plain incompetent, enumerating the pros and cons of both types of temperament. The sub-inspector thought he used the same technique in his classes. Digressions allowed a few seconds' rest, both to him and to the students taking notes and then he could go back with greater emphasis to his theme, focus and make students focus on what was essential.

"When I received your e-mail asking me to come to your office," said Bellpuig, "I thought you wanted to ask me about the disappeared Romanian student and I didn't even imagine that Laura Cremona had also vanished and that nothing had been known of her since the television interview which I had watched with Domenica. Last Friday evening after the TV news, looking for further facts about Laura's death, I called Rosa Casasaies, but I got her voice mail and decided not to leave a message in case my colleague returned my call at an inconvenient time. I was glad I did not because at that moment, I got a call on my cell. It was Mònica, telling me she was downstairs and needed to know my room number. Opening the door, I noticed she wore makeup and a very fetching tight-fitting dress. 'You are trying to make up for last Friday, aren't you? I can tell,' I told her and gave her a hug. Mònica said that the Autònoma had become highly dangerous and if it hadn't been for fear of upsetting me, she would have called that afternoon to tell me to meet her in Barcelona. She said that it was time to break the tradition of meeting at the Serhs – something she had originally insisted on – until we found out whether the student under arrest who was a school friend of the victim, was the murderer or not. She said his name was Bru. I couldn't believe it; he wasn't my student, but I knew him. With Laura and Domenica, he was part of the triad in charge of finding Iliescu. I had spoken with him …Mònica had heard on the radio that besides Bru, there was another person in custody. What had happened on campus seemed to excite her even more than our furtive meetings. I had a horrible night, sleepless. The hours crawled on. If Monica had not minded my leaving her alone, I would have gone to Domenica's. When Mònica woke up around seven in the morning, she found me showered and dressed. I wanted to gain time and go see Domenica as soon as Monica left. Fortunately, the Vila is next door to the hotel. I didn't mind arriving two hours before the time I'd told her. I didn't care if I got her out of bed or if she was with someone. I had a dreadful feeling."

"What kind of feeling?" the sub-inspector asked. She doubted the truth of all his explanations.

"That whoever had killed Laura would also want to kill Domenica and I might still be in time to prevent it."

"I see!" Manuela exclaimed, unable to contain her surprise at Bellpuig's words. "What did you do then?"

"I settled the hotel bill and ran to Domenica's place. From the street I rang the apartment. There was no answer. But I was lucky and didn't need to insist. A girl with a suitcase who was leaving the building let me in. I ran up to the third floor and rang again, but no answer. I thought Domenica might be sleeping or out and decided to go have some breakfast and return at the appointed hour. Perhaps she had spent the night at a friend's and would come back at ten as we had agreed."

"Did you ring a few times?"

"I think so."

"And you didn't notice the door was ajar and the lock had been forced?"

"No," Bellpuig said, disconcerted. "I saw nothing strange."

Manuela Vázquez asked to be excused for a second. She wanted to check something. She got her cell phone and dialed: "Good evening, Inspector," she said. "Can you give me the number of agent Cañizares? I need to know at what moment the neighbors noticed the door had been forced. Professor Bellpuig assures me that when he went to the girl's apartment…oh, yeah, they were to have breakfast together, the door was locked. He rang and no one opened…thanks, Inspector. See you."

The sub-inspector dialed another number.

"Hi, Cañizares. It's Manuel Vázquez. Besides the veterinary student, who else saw the door had been forced? You know the time? Thanks. Let me write it down."

Manuela Vázquez jotted down on a piece of paper the data she was given and then, addressing Bellpuig, she spoke in an ironic tone: "Two students have stated that when they came back from a night in town, about five in the morning on Sunday, they saw the door had been forced. But I don't know how reliable they are. You went there later, is that not so? And the door was locked, right?"

"Yes, I am sure. It was around seven, seven-thirty, I told you, but that was the morning of Saturday, not the night between Saturday and Sunday."

"And what did you do then?" She asked curtly.

"I went back to the hotel to finally have my first coffee of the day and checked my e-mail to find out if Domenica had decided against seeing me and in fact, I had a message. She had sent it on Friday evening. She was postponing the meeting until Tuesday because she wanted to get out of Bellaterra for the weekend. I was sorry not to see her, but the fact that she had gone away relaxed me. Then I got on the train to Barcelona."

"But unfortunately, Domenica did not leave," the sub-inspector said in a vigorous voice, looking Bellpuig in the eye.

30

Sub-Inspector Vázquez let Professor Bellpuig go and told him she would probably call on him again. She trusted he wouldn't leave the area as he did last week and could be found in his house or at the university. He assured her he was at her disposal and then she requested his cell phone number. She had those of his home and office, as well as that of an old, useless cell which never got picked up – she had called that number quite a few times. It was the number given by the university when she requested the data of all the professors who taught classes with Erasmus scholars enrolled.

There was something about Professor Bellpuig that Manuela Vázquez didn't like. She couldn't quite put her finger on it. It could be his exaggerated willingness to cooperate with the police or his way of explaining his relationship with "Mònica," whose actual name he refused to give, claiming he did not want to compromise her. Of course, sooner or later, the police would have to get it, as she was his alibi. In addition to all this, he lied. It was impossible that his sentence had coincided with that of her namesake, the writer in the Lleida prison. She was familiar with Manolo Vázquez Montalbán's life and deeds; he was imprisoned in 1962 when Bellpuig, born in 1953, would have been nine. They could in no way have been cell-mates. Why did he claim that? Why was he lying? Was Bellpuig the murderer? They had no proof, but the fact he had slept in Bellaterra on both Fridays could not be disregarded. As soon as the informatics team from the forensic department had sent the e-mails exchanged by Domenica and Bellpuig, she checked to see if they matched what he had told her, which she had taped with the tiny and sophisticated recorder inserted in her pen. She knew that such recording, not authorized by a judge, was useless in court, but it allowed her to verify what the professor had admitted was not what she would have liked him to say. The e-mails matched, but not one hundred percent and besides, the one in which Domenica canceled her meeting with Bellpuig was missing. No such thing was in the e-mails sent by the girl.

Regarding those they had recovered, the sub-inspector quickly realized that Domenica's "Professor Bellpuig, I need to speak with you urgently," sent on 4th December 2008, the very day she had given the police his name when she told them he had spent the night in her apartment, had one single intent: to explain to him that she had to reveal his name. She wanted to tell Bellpuig in person and not in writing and in a language she hadn't quite mastered.

His, on the other hand, was much more suggestive: "My dear, I am away from Barcelona, I will be back Friday night at the Bellaterra hotel. I am delighted you want to speak with me. I'll drop by your place; if I can't on Friday, then Saturday morning around ten. Yours, Carles." One could conclude that Bellpuig was fantasizing about delights more tactile and within reach, a continuation of the fun time he'd had the previous weekend. The sub-inspector did not fail to notice that Bellpuig wrote about seeing the student also Friday night. Why then had he told her only about Saturday?

Manuela Vázquez dialed Lluc's number. She wanted him to ask the Hotel Serhs receptionist for the exact times when Bellpuig came in and left, both on Friday 28th and Friday 5th. She also asked him if they had run the fingerprints through the system, but the corporal did not know yet and gave her the number of the forensic department.

Fifteen minutes later, she got a fax with the information she had requested. On Friday 28th, Bellpuig had signed in at 7:40 p.m. and had checked out at 11:45 a.m. On Friday 5th he had arrived at 8:14 p.m. and left very early at 7:30 on Saturday morning. He had requested a room with a double bed, but they couldn't tell her if he'd slept there alone or not since they had no other registered guest for the room. In any case, the Serhs' front desk, as in most hotels, only required one ID per room. The woman hidden under the name "Mònica" might again have failed to meet Bellpuig and he had spent the night with Domenica. If this were the case, there were quite a few points in favor of his being the murderer. But why kill her? Was it a game? A game that increased orgasmic enjoyment? And did both Laura and Domenica agree to play? Even when Domenica knew what had happened to Laura? Was this what it was all about? In this case, Bellpuig's seductive powers must be limitless, such an ostentatiously learned type, so keen on cooperating...

The phone rang.

"Lluçanès here. What's that saying about the Prophet and the mountain? I know Bellpuig left not long ago because his lawyer just called me. He says the professor is alleging intimidation. What did you do to him, Sub-Inspector? Did you bite him or did you tickle him? Or make him sit on a whoopee cushion? You absolutely can't do this kind of thing. You'll get a reprimand larger than a grand piano. Bellpuig is powerful, very powerful. You didn't know that already?"

Lluçanès's mocking tone relieved the sub-inspector's uneasiness. She had been startled by the intimidation claim. She was lucky to have the unauthorized recording to prove that she had behaved as if she were a member of the court at Versailles, with extreme *politesse*. More relaxed she said: "No, I didn't know. And what makes him so powerful, besides writing books and lecturing on paintings?"

"His brother is the personal adviser to the president. They say he has more power than a cabinet member."

"Then you'll understand, Inspector, that I don't care. If he is guilty we'll do all we can for the judge to sentence him to prison, you can be sure of that. He will be given the same treatment as we gave Bru. We do not value degrees or anything of the kind. We do not treat professors different from students. And who is his lawyer?"

"Ernest Civera, one of the best. He has been president of the Bar Association."

"And what's his problem?"

"He claims you have interrogated his client to trick him into saying things that might make him a suspect, using the old methods...It's always the same. That next time he will be the one to determine what Senor Bellpuig will or will not say."

"You know what? This makes me think that Bellpuig is not innocent. Our meeting today was an exchange of impressions and not a formal interrogation. Let him make no mistake." And changing the topic: "What do we know about the fingerprints?"

"There are tons of them: those from the security patrol that searched for the victim's papers, those of the medics the patrol guys called and who got there before us, but also those of our important professor, and these are relevant. But I have to hang up now; I must rush to the Forensic Anatomical Institute. I imagine you don't want to go there yourself, for I'd be more than happy to let you do it."

31

The task of informing Domenica Arrigo's parents that their daughter was dead, fell on Dante Braccalente. Late in the morning of Sunday, 7th December, he dialed the phone number Manuela Vázquez had given him. This time he did not think of a line of poetry, but tried to find some religious reference, supposing the Arrigos being from southern Italy, must be devout Catholics who would be helped by the consolation faith affords before such fearsome misfortune. He got it right; the cries of Domenica's mother, who answered the phone call, were filled with references to God; how could He allow such a fate for her *angelo*? Why did the Lord place such a burden on her? She was a good Catholic, a good housewife and mother, she went to mass every Sunday. Why did God want to test her so?

During their conversation, the consul glossed over the more macabre aspects of the murder and reiterated that the police were about to arrest the criminal. He learned that Domenica was the third of five children of a mechanic, the owner of a small workshop and of an administrative employee from an electronics distribution business. Even though she was familiar with the Internet and a devotee of computers – she used to Skype with her daughter often and also e-mailed her – Signora Arrigo was a traditional woman, most devout, a trait that comforted the consul. There was no better medicine to alleviate the pain of such losses than the consolation of religion. To think that Domenica waited for her in heaven where they would be reunited, was less punishing than thinking she would never again see her daughter. It was not the same thing to face death with the certainty of an afterlife than to do so thinking that all ended here, that there was nothing beyond.

The rector had asked the consul to offer Domenica's parents tickets to fly to Barcelona and to pay for the hotel nights they would need until they could take their daughter's body home. They accepted, but requested to travel only once the authorities gave them permission to bring the body home. They had no desire to wait for the bureaucratic paperwork in a city that they had looked forward to visiting with Domenica to show them around. From now on, the city would be forever hateful to them.

Braccalente left them his office phone number and also his cell's, which was like another organ to him he told them, since he had it on his person at all times. He also promised to keep them informed of the police investigations and would alert them when they could take the remains of their hapless Domenica to Naples.

Dante Braccalente was downcast. Feeling increasingly sure that the murderer belonged to the young women's circle, he contacted the director of the Italian Institute to inquire of his personnel who could have interacted with Laura and Domenica during the past few months. Francesco Gregoti told him the police had asked for the same thing that very morning, not even two hours ago. He would see to it, but they would have to wait until Tuesday; Monday was a holiday and the Institute was closed.

The consul attempted to invite Signore Cremona-Hogarth to dinner, but they declined. Domenica's death saddened them deeply and they preferred to remain at the hotel. They weren't hungry. Neither was the consul, so vital and *gourmand* normally; this was a grim sign. It meant that the degree of his concern was extreme. So extreme, in fact, that he spent the whole afternoon trying to figure out if the death of the two Italian Erasmus scholars might have been decreed long distance by some mafia gang and their hired assassin. They ought to investigate the family backgrounds of Laura and Domenica.

It was clear there were no ties, economic or otherwise, between the two families, that the only link was the friendship between the daughters. He suspected that revenge would be aimed at the Arrigos who lived in Naples and not at Signora Cremona who lived in Milan. That Laura had been killed first was a mistake; they were after Domenica. This conclusion seemed logical to him and he called Sub-Inspector Vázquez to let her know. He thought it could make for a good starting point and suggested they contact the Italian police who could be efficient at times.

The sub-inspector shared with Lluçanès the consul's conjectures. The inspector said he had already contacted the Italian police. He had thought of that possibility also. Mafia reprisals were characterized by their cruelty. If they wanted to punish one of the families, they could well choose to kill the girls, two for the price of one. They had to wait for the Italian police investigation, but on principle, they discarded any links between the Arrigos, the Cremonas and the mafia. This strengthened the sub-inspector's hypothesis; she had a candidate: Professor Bellpuig.

Late as it was, Manuela asked Professor Casasaies if she could see her for a minute and speak about her colleague, especially of his relations with students. She wanted to have all possible references about the man before requesting a judge's order to interrogate him formally. She thought that Rosa's insights would be a great help. Since it was Sunday and after 8 o'clock at night, the sub-inspector didn't think she could ask Rosa to come to Cerdanyola and so offered to meet her in Barcelona at the bar of the Hotel Casa Fuster near Rosa's home. She promised it would not take long.

At 8:40 p.m., Manuela walked into the hotel; Rosa had just arrived. With a cup of tea and a margarita that a waiter served them right away, they looked like two friends trying to drown the evening's tedium together and not like a stressed out policewoman and professor. Manuela, after insisting on the utmost discretion, told Rosa that Carles Bellpuig had an affair with one of the murdered students.

The professor smiled in an odd way, both melancholy and ironic. She knew her colleague well; years ago, her sister, Glòria, had been one of his "victims." She didn't have to explain the sense of the word for Vázquez to get it right away.

"Glòria was promoted from student to secretary," Rosa said, "a post the whole class vied for. Yet, not only was it a non-paying job, but often, the secretaries had to buy the books or photocopies Bellpuig requested with their own money. However, this didn't matter to them. To be Bellpuig's chosen one was the best thing that could happen to you. It meant that at the end of the service, you would be assured an assistantship. Of course, then you had more work; you had to draft articles that he signed, but barely revised and work on the monumental *Dictionary of Art Terms* that so helped his career because it carried his name as the only author, as though he never had any help, even though a bunch of idiots had burned their eyes for a couple of years, also without remuneration or even a word of thanks. To be part of his team meant an entry into the country's university elite and the certainty of belonging to the right crowd: to the left of the Left. Bellpuig was a militant and the leader in a minority faction, a splinter group from the communist Bandera Roja. It was rumored that he'd been imprisoned, but he neither agreed with nor denied the rumor, saying dismissively that 'personal matters are irrelevant' or 'we must all sacrifice for our country's freedom.' His acolytes praised such modesty which they thought extraordinary, even though it did not go with his almighty ego. He often held forth on the ideals that would make the Autònoma a unique university, but those ideals boiled down to stereotyped conventions, just like the ones he boasted to oppose: pure formulas, flashes in the pan. Bellpuig was one of the professors who fought against having a commencement ceremony; those things were bourgeois pretences that did not fit their university's spirit and neither did caps and gowns…Now, all this seems laughable. Does it make us more progressive to deny our students – many of them first-generation college students – a graduation ceremony and yet endorse an end-of-the-year party that would end in drunken blackouts? At the time, all that Bellpuig did or said became dogma to his followers because his person radiated a special magnetism and he upheld his ideas with great vigor. But he has changed with time. Nowadays, he is a standard bearer for order. He addresses his students formally and is against the occupiers, something unthinkable in the past. As for women..."

Rosa Casasaies paused, took a sip of her cocktail, and went on: "Women...if he fancied you, he could be the world's greatest seducer until you agreed to go to bed with him. Charming and persuasive, he conquered not by revealing his strength but his weakness. It was up to you; if you didn't love him he was rendered useless, even his classes went awry...he'd bring you flowers, daisies; I suppose roses seemed too bourgeois to him, not to mention their higher price tag, and he wrote you poems. Once his interest in his 'victim' began to wane (I know this because it cost my sister a deep depression) he saw nothing wrong in revealing every painful detail. But this is an old story and unfortunately, my sister cannot speak about it. She died from ovarian cancer when she was still young...if you want to know if he's bedded the foreign students, ask him; he'll probably say he did, although they might have rejected him."

"Not a paragon of virtue, it seems," the sub-inspector said.

"I may not be the most appropriate person to judge him. You should speak with other colleagues. He still has his followers, but they are fewer. He's had problems with the research team he leads. His assistant is fed up with him, he can't stand the constant humiliations. He's probably afraid to confront him because, as was the case with my sister, he must still admire him. I told you he exerts a kind of magnetism over people. Since he is not all that interested in his scholarly career right now, he has taken to flattering politicians, regardless of their affiliations. He aspires to a position outside of the Autònoma."

"Such as?"

"Director of the IVAM, the Institut Valencià d'Art Modern. He has ties to València; his family is from that area. This is why, recently during an interview, he seemed to be buttering up Rita Barberà and her conservative party."

32

On Monday, 8th December at 10 o'clock in the morning, Lluçanès again gathered his team in the conference room. First, he inquired about Rosario Hurtado's health; she had left the hospital the day before to return to work and he welcomed her back. Then, addressing the group, he added that since he had them work without rest from Saturday on, not allowing them to take a day's off for either Constitution Day or the Immaculate Virgin holiday, he had decided to offer them coffee, orange juice and pastries and pointed to a table where the breakfast foods were assembled. He wanted to lift their spirits, he told them. After what had happened, he understood they might feel despondent, which was not good. They had to make every possible effort to solve the case soon and they would accomplish that with a good dose of optimism. All eyes were on them; it was up to them and only them to bring back the lost calm to the campus. Their responsibility was great; the citizens would trust the mossos if they saw they had captured the perpetrator.

The sub-inspector suspected that Lluçanès had practiced his little speech in front of his bathroom mirror after shaving and rubbing some after-shave lotion on his cheeks, the scent of which was still noticeable. She wondered whether the performance he offered them would fit a scene in an American TV movie or a chapter in a self-help manual meant for the Mossos d'Esquadra. But as soon as the inspector went from those few minutes of rhetoric to concrete aspects, Manuela

Vázquez dropped her note-taking and listened to him with all her being.

The order of the day, the inspector said as he sat down, consisted of two items only. First, to bring to the table the results of the individual investigations and second, to derive the pertinent conclusions leading to the arrest of the murderer. On his part, he had received the autopsy report on Domenica and he would summarize its most salient aspects. He did not read it, however. He disliked the terms the doctors used because doctors, by the mere use of an arcane vocabulary, felt superior. He would limit himself to pointing out the key findings: "Domenica died in the early hours of Saturday between four and five o' clock exactly one week after Laura's death. She was attacked in her bed, as no sign has been found that her body was dragged or transported from another spot. She was probably asleep when she was strangled and could not defend herself. No residue of alien skin has been found under her nails and no bruises or scratches on her arms. The murderer used a scarf and just like in Laura's case, left it wrapped around the victim's neck. I believe," Lluçanès added, "that the scarf was the one Domenica wore in the photographs that you, Rosario, found in Bru's apartment. The girl might have left it with other clothes on a chair."

The inspector went on to say that one of the details that most baffled the examiner and himself was the macabre calling card left by the murderer: the plastic cockroach he had placed under the tongue of his victim. He asked Rifà if he could offer anything new on this point and the agent said there were several companies that marketed such objects online and passed on a bunch of images he had printed to see if any of them matched the one found in Domenica's mouth. He also attempted to figure out a relationship between the cockroach and the mouse found on Laura's body: both animals had to do with death. The killer might have left them to stress the fact that the girls were dead and that death had come to them by his hand. In his opinion, the murderer was a sadist. First thing the next morning, he told them with a grimace, he would visit the stores that sold those repugnant gadgets and share his findings.

A pale Rosario Hurtado, looking tired, dressed in a uniform that seemed loose on her, spoke after Rifà as she was seated next to him and it was customary during those meetings to proceed clockwise around the table, starting with the first person to be given the floor. Yesterday afternoon, she had checked Bru's alibi. Since being freed by the judge, he'd been at his parents' in Vilanova, in bed with the flu and had seen a doctor who had prescribed complete rest. Rosario had managed to verify that the guy's temperature was not the kind that the teenagers of her time used as an excuse to skip school, but a real fever. With such a high temperature, it was impossible for him to have gone to Bellaterra to kill Domenica. And if both deaths were the work of one assassin, as seemed the case, they'd have to discard Bru.

"I'm sure we gave him the flu," the sub-inspector quipped. "There's no heating in our cells." Manuela Vázquez found Bru unpalatable and so she allowed herself the sarcasm that seemed out of line to Hurtado, but the agent didn't dare respond.

"And what about the girl's neighbors, Cañizares?" Lluçanès asked "You've spoken with them, haven't you?"

"Yes, sir," Cañizares said. He was the one agent who was not in uniform. He wore a leather jacket, a red turtleneck and those blue jeans that are new but full of rips and tears. He had chosen the outfit to look like a student and walk around the campus more at ease. "I believe I've spoken with all who were there; some neighbors, it seems, have gone away for the long weekend and will be coming back today. I'll head over there after this meeting. I haven't contacted the folks in the apartment next to the girls' yet — biology students, I've been told — or the three other neighbors from the first floor. All the tenants I've spoken to said they heard nothing out of the ordinary; the sounds of steps and doors closing were normal for a Saturday morning. There were also some little visits across the hall to share drinks and joints. But there is no unanimity when it comes to the forced door which only the neighbors on the same floor could have seen."

"Or her visitors," Corporal Lluc added. Cañizares always made him nervous; he tended to go off on tangents.

"I was about to mention that," a somewhat cross Cañizares said. "Around one o' clock during the night between Friday and Saturday, some boys went up to meet some girls on the third floor, third door, but they got the wrong apartment and knocked on the second door. A girl opened; judging from their description it must have been Domenica. They saw they'd gotten the wrong apartment because their little friends weren't there; there was only an elderly gentleman sitting there, smoking. They thought he was the girl's father. They saw him again when leaving around three o' clock because he was also leaving. The door was not forced at that hour; they heard it closing. The sound of the latch is unmistakable."

"I imagine you've localized the boys," Lluçanès said. "Sub-Inspector, we need a photograph of your suspect right away. Do you have one?"

"Not here, but we can get one from the Internet. All we need is a computer and a good printer."

"Go to my office. Give me a second to alert my secretary or rather, if you all excuse me, I'll come with you."

Lluçanès left the room to go to his office, followed by Manuela.

"If it's Bellpuig, the director-general will croak and the rector will kill himself," he told her. "If you don't mind, accompany Cañizares, talk to the boys and dispel any doubts. Do you think he is capable of murder?"

"It's hard for me to imagine he could be so crazy. What I am sure of, however, is that he's not telling us the whole truth."

33

While the discovery of Laura's body had affected everybody and most especially the students, professors and administrators in the School of Letters, the news of her friend Domenica's death, which could not be kept under wraps and which the media began to spread on Monday, unleashed panic all over Bellaterra. On Tuesday, 9th December, since the university had suspended all academic activities as a sign of mourning, very few students attended the events in memory of Laura and Domenica. Some of the anti-Bologna strikers in attendance displayed a banner protesting Iliescu's disappearance. Their leader, Miquel Oliver, berated the dean and complained there was no mention of Iliescu which he attributed to "class," the same reason so frequently brought up in their assemblies. But the protesters had the rug pulled from under their feet when the vice-rector for International Affairs informed them that Iliescu had not disappeared and insisted – presenting his hypothetical trip to Romania as an indisputable fact – that the student had gone back to his home country freely as he himself had mentioned in an e-mail.

Marcel Bru, escorted by a girl who looked at him with stars in her eyes, sat amid the protesters. His arrival had been received with an ovation. His arrest had turned him into a hero in the eyes of some of the students. The flu that had kept him in bed had made his skin even yellower. He seemed ill, but not wanting to miss the homage to his friends only added to his credit in the eyes of his peers.

The group that really did not want to miss the event was the swarm of journalists. The novelty of the news generated by the two Erasmus scholars lured them more speedily than a horse's ass lures flies. "We are not used to such horrors here," one of the many chroniclers was saying before a camera. "This is not the United States where this sort of thing is normal. But now, besides the ketchup, burgers and sneakers that have been invading us for years, it seems we are also importing the fashion of campus murders."

The caution and discretion requested by the police had evaporated and the insistence upon freedom of the press had won the day; with this freedom, audience ratings improved. When even the national newscasters took as their mantra that a death brought spice to the news program, what could be expected from the sensationalist programs that could provide such morbidly juicy reports? The supposedly serious press devoted full-page spreads to the murders. Some columnists, after blaming the university in general, pointed the finger at the academic authorities. Others went even further; it was the Erasmus adviser who, if she had any dignity, should resign from her post. Others simply called for the resignation of the rector's team. Since Domenica's body was found on Sunday, the rector had created a permanent crisis council including other members of the faculty. Aware of the media tsunami that was about to engulf them as soon as the news of the second body spread, the group instructed the head of communications to prepare a couple of memos. They knew that a consensus would not come easy because not everyone in the rector's team thought the same way. Some thought that the Autònoma's prestige had never fallen so low and that the only way out was the rector's resignation and a call for advanced elections. Others thought this would make the situation much worse, as it would reveal incompetence and cowardice beyond compare in the history of the university.

During the memorial, those who upheld the first opinion, made it public. If the rector had not emphasized that the event was meant to remember the two students they had lost, the people in attendance would have engaged in a deeply counterproductive academic free-for-all.

Manuela Vázquez, accompanied by Rosario Hurtado who had insisted on attending the memorial for the two girls, sat in the last row. They'd been among the first to go into the auditorium, but they remained there, near the door because the sub-inspector wanted to see if Bellpuig would attend. Soon after the adviser for the Erasmus students began to speak – an emotional Rosa Casasaies sounded dejected and in evoking Domenica, she no longer could hold her tears and sobs – Bellpuig came in. Keeping a low profile, he walked down the steps and sat in the middle of the room, near the aisle.

"Let's keep our eyes on him," Manuela Vázquez told Rosario. "If he leaves, follow him and keep me posted. I'll stay until the end of the ceremony, but I won't leave without him."

The sub-inspector had the court order allowing her to interrogate and detain the professor as a suspect. Once the friends of Domenica's next-door neighbors had recognized him, she wanted them to identify him. The police also needed samples of his DNA to find out whether the traces of bodily fluids found in the girl's vagina were his.

Rosario rose when she saw Bellpuig getting up and went to the door to wait for him outside, but he didn't leave by that exit. He climbed up to the stage, handed a folder to the students' representative and went backstage. "Maybe he's preparing a presentation on the students," Manuela thought, "and is now getting it ready." It had been a mistake not to get a copy of the memorial's order of service in advance. But she was so overworked. She texted Rosario and told her to check the other exit to see if Bellpuig had gone that way. The agent went there and after fifteen minutes of fruitless waiting, asked Manuela via text whether the professor had reentered the auditorium; Manuela texted back that he hadn't. Then, Rosario, pretending she knew no better, got in through the back door which led to the stage and to two rooms by a passageway. One was a kind of dressing room and the other looked like a storage room. They were both empty.

"I've lost him, I'm sorry," she keyed in and sent the message to Manuela. A few seconds later, she received the sub-inspector's message: "Go to his office."

Rosario had been to the school before, but she still had to ask where the offices of the art faculty were. "Second floor," some students told her, pointing at a stairway. They were carrying bags of food and seemed to belong to the horde of occupiers. Upstairs, she saw classrooms and offices. She read the names by the doors one by one and their office hours, but found no reference to Bellpuig. In the corridor, she ran into a tall young woman with long fluffy hair and dark glasses and asked her if she knew the whereabouts of Professor Bellpuig's office in the Department of Art. She shook her head and pointed at her throat as if unable to speak. Rosario got her notebook from her bag and a pen from her coat's pocket and offered them to her. Without removing her gloves, the young woman wrote, "I've lost my voice, sorry. I think the art offices are one floor up on the other side," and walked on.

Rosario Hurtado went back down and crossed the lobby to reach the other part of the building. She went up to the second floor, but found only the offices of the Geography Department and not those of the Art Department. Annoyed at not finding Bellpuig's office, she went downstairs again. She decided she'd better go to the main office to get directions. As a matter of fact, the woman had pointed her in the opposite direction. She went down again, turned right, went up one floor and proceeded once more. When she turned around the corner of the corridor, she saw other offices, Bellpuig's among them. She knocked on the door. There was no answer. She knocked louder, but it was still in vain. She then tried the door to see if it was unlocked and the door gave way. What she saw there made her take a few steps back and let out a startled cry.

Rosario Hurtado felt sick to her stomach and was afraid she might throw up right there and then. She rushed out of the office and vomited near the door. She wiped her mouth with a Kleenex and called Manuela. She could barely speak. Her legs shook and her heart raced. She vacillated between going downstairs and waiting there for the sub-inspector. She felt ashamed to let Manuela see the extent of her loss of self-control and looked for a bathroom. She recalled having seen one near the stairs to the Art Department and ran across, pulled out a couple of yards of toilet paper, wet it and returning to Bellpuig's office door, cleaned up her vomit, grimacing all the time. When Manuela Vázquez arrived, Rosario could barely speak.

"This has just happened, Sub-Inspector, and I think I have seen the culprit. It's a woman; she's got no voice and has written this." She showed her superior the note.

34

On Wednesday, 10th December, almost all news programs opened with the same tragic announcement which was also summarized in newspaper headlines. Some emphasized the feelings of sadness for the loss: "Consternation in Catalan University Circles," "Dismay in Catalonia," "Deep Sorrow," or "Desolation and Distress in the Classrooms"; others stressed such things as "Murderous Brutality." There had been three deaths until that moment, and with the murderer still at large, who knew if there wouldn't be more?

Many TV stations had sent mobile units to the campus and since the police prevented them from entering the area of the Art Department's offices, they took to interviewing students, professors and staff willing to offer an opinion. There were TV and radio units from Catalonia and other parts of Spain, and also European reporters. Most of these came from Italy not only because the dead Erasmus students were Italian but also because the TV program heads of that country, under the control of Berlusconi, considered academic blood a lure to attract viewership.

The university authorities had decreed suspension of classes for three days of mourning, postponing activities until the following week. They had also decided not to call a press conference. The police did not want to issue any statements either, maintaining that silence was one of the best weapons to find the perpetrator of the crimes and sooner or later, by whatever means, deliver him to justice.

The institutional silence had to do more with the shock provoked by Bellpuig's death among the faculty members who had been directly involved with the case than with the need to avoid interfering with the mossos' job. The rector's team had decided to resign and call for advance elections. The rector and the vice-rectors on the team fantasized about a sabbatical year which they would spend far from the campus. The distance of a year might help them erase the memories of those ill-fated days, assuming that things would stop there and that there would be no further crimes. But nobody could guarantee that the murderer, still at large, would not strike again.

At the university, all conversations ended up making reference to the horrors witnessed, and many students were curious about the relationship that had existed among the three victims and why they had been chosen by the murderer. Some hypothesized that if the criminal had killed two female students, perhaps he would kill two professors to balance things and then two members of the administrative personnel and service staff. The murderer might be quite the democratic type, but who was he? Who could, with such impunity, punish them so brutally? And why wasn't he caught? Why did the mossos seem at sea? Was it one murderer or several? Were they following orders? Was it a serial killer or a paid assassin?

That Bellpuig had been professor for both dead Erasmus scholars put his colleagues who also taught the women on guard, especially Rosa Casasaies who was also their adviser. She could well be the next victim. She was sure that the murderer knew her, that he knew all of them, for he was a member of the community. The dean, equally frightened, had taken leave and locked herself in her home. In an extraordinarily crazed state, she did nothing but produce careless translations into Latin; she found it extremely hard to express in such a noble classical language the stress that had overcome her and to which her bowels reacted with flatulence and diarrhea.

Bellpuig's murder, which implied his innocence, a condition Manuela Vázquez had not seen as quite clear, provoked a flood of obituaries. Reading them, the sub-inspector had the impression that what Rosa Casasaies had told her about the assistants he had employed, especially when it came to working on the dictionary, was not true. All the notices insisted that Bellpuig, by himself, without helpers, had prepared the most important *Dictionary of Art Terms* and had done a large part of the work during his politically fuelled imprisonment. Who was speaking the truth? Where was the evidence?

Manuela Vázquez had grown increasingly happy with the profession she'd chosen where you checked the facts scrupulously using scientific methods. This compensated for the erroneous suppositions which often gave rise to them. Unfortunately, with the case at hand, the few facts they had weren't getting them very far: the biological remnants found in Laura's vagina came from Marcel Bru; there was no doubt about this. And the sub-inspector had just learned from DNA testing that those the examiner had found on Domenica's body came from Bellpuig. As for fingerprints, these were diverse and dispersed – from Bru's cousin's car, from Domenica's apartment and from Bellpuig's office. The forensic folks were convinced the murderer had worn gloves.

In the case of the girls, the murder weapons – the muffler and scarf – had not been removed from the bodies, but with Bellpuig, much as they looked, they never found one. From the gash on the professor head, the police gathered that the weapon must have been a blunt object: a hammer, a wrench or pliers. Or perhaps even a rock. If, as it seemed, he'd been caught by surprise as he sat at his desk facing his computer, the aggressor, if it was someone tall with long arms, would have had no difficulty in striking as soon as he entered because the desk was rather narrow and the office quite small.

The examiner, Golorons, once again explained to Lluçanès' satisfaction that the blow had been delivered from the right side of the body and very forcefully. This suggested that the perpetrator was a tall and strong person and possibly left-handed. The perpetrator had then pulled on Bellpuig's tie, tightening it around his neck to finish the job. This fact and the plastic fly he had placed in the palm of Bellpuig's right hand, connected the three deaths with a similar imprint. And what could they learn from all that? That the murderer was laughing at them, while the police stood completely baffled, understanding nothing.

35

From the rector on, down to the last janitor hired by the cleaning subcontractors, everyone was counting the days left until the Christmas break. The holidays would provide the oxygen they all needed to breathe easier and regain a normal rhythm in their lives. For those most given to hypochondria like the dean and Rosa Casasaies, the pulsations of their hearts felt like symptoms of an imminent heart attack. The rector had requested police protection for them as soon as Bellpuig's body had been found, since the two women, more than anyone else, had some relationship with the dead girls. But the Erasmus adviser was not so anxious for herself as for her daughter, a student in the Autònoma's Information Science Department, intent on going up to Bellaterra and returning home alone late at night. She was also furious with her parents who always tried to control her as she kept saying and who had now found a perfect reason to do so.

Rosa Casasaies was quite depressed by the tension with her daughter who often gave her parents the silent treatment. She shut herself in her room and left it only for meals. Rosa felt she would never again recover the sweet girl her daughter used to be before the puberty hormones began to ooze from her, making her aloof and self-centered. She often wondered what wrong she'd done. Now her guilt was aggravated by a new obsession: that the campus murderer would choose her daughter to inflict an even greater pain on her.

Her husband tried to calm her down. "The campus murderer," he would say, "doesn't know if you have a daughter or not, he is not an omniscient God." On the other hand, he was concerned about Rosa. The best she could do, Albert insisted, was to leave Barcelona, go to Pals and rest.

Rosa, however, wanted to make sure as she did every night, that Cristina was back home asleep in her room. Besides, she couldn't abide being by herself. Bellpuig's death had moved her to open old wounds she believed had healed. Now the wounds had propelled her back to the time when the man had gone after her. She didn't dare confess this to the sub-inspector and had invented the affair between Bellpuig and her dead sister, projecting her own experience. It had been a brief siege, a couple of weeks, enough for her to yield to his desire. She had many fantasies about that moment. It was her first time and she had imagined she'd even hear celestial music. Nothing like that happened. Bellpuig fucked her in his car, quite near the campus, in a little-frequented Bellaterra subdivision where he probably often took his victims. Returning to Barcelona, he didn't even take her home. He dropped her off at the first metro station they found on the way:

"I'm in a hurry, sweetheart. I am expected at the committee meeting."

Just as he said goodbye, she knew his interest in her had ended. She felt so humiliated, so used and so ashamed that she swore never to tell anyone that she'd lost her virginity to Bellpuig. That was one of the memories she would have wanted to erase or rather, what she would have liked to erase was the fact itself, as if it had never taken place. That was why she resorted to not thinking about it and managed to put it out of her mind. She passed Bellpuig in the school's corridors as though there had never been an intimate relationship between them. Neither of them ever mentioned the time when she was his pet student. With the same obsessive insistence with which he had pursued her, he stopped talking to her the moment he added her name to the list of offerings at the altar of his formidable ego.

Bellpuig's funeral, which took place at the Les Corts mortuary two days after his killing, became a social event attended by the president of the Generalitat, cabinet members, city councilmen, two directors-general from Madrid as government representatives, leaders from all political parties and friends and acquaintances by the dozen. There were speeches and a musical tribute. Rosa Casasaies wept, as did other female professors and some males, as well as his woeful assistant who appeared even more dejected and stunned. Out of respect for the deceased, he had removed his hat with which he hid a scar on his scalp, the result, he said, of his having been hit by a door. With bandaged head, he appeared both ridiculous and pitiful. His oink-like sobs were quite eerie and prevented his reading in full the half page he had penned with references to the latest work his master had prepared on Baroque *vanitates*.

Rosa cried a little for the dead man, some more for what that third murder implied and the rest for herself, for what she had been and no longer was, for what Bellpuig meant, for the five minutes when he'd become her first lover and for the two long years of her love for him, the first in her life. She cried as she remembered the evenings by the phone, hoping for a call from Bellpuig, her movements at the university as she tried to catch him along some passageway...but her attack of self-pity lasted only a short while. As she looked at her female colleagues, she felt solidarity, suspecting that some of them might have had similar experiences.

osario Hurtado was obsessed with the idea that the woman who had misdirected her away from Bellpuig's office was the one who had killed him, a theory only Manuela Vázquez took seriously. Lluçanès, on the other hand, argued that giving someone the wrong directions did not make them a suspect. Didn't Rosario herself mention that all the modules in the School of Letters looked alike? But as he did not want to discard any possibility, however slight, he sent the agent to the composite picture bureau. Rosario described the voiceless girl: tall and rather brawny, dressed in a loose-fitting jacket, dark pants and brown boots. Rosario hadn't seen her eyes because the stranger hid them behind large dark glasses. Long, disheveled blond tresses, surely the result of a straw-colored dye or perhaps a wig, covered part of her heavily made-up face. The most important features she remembered were a prominent jaw, a well-proportioned nose and fleshy lips. According to her colleagues specializing in composite portraits, the woman's description reminded them of Iliescu's picture on the flyers. The conclusions of one of the graphologists also pointed to the student. He thought the handwriting from the essay found on Bellpuig's desk had traits similar to the note in the agent's notebook. Another thought the similarity was not indicative and insisted there were more features in common with Bellpuig's scribbled note of "good interpretation" – and Bellpuig was the victim, not the murderer – than with Iliescu's hand. They had no other leads, however. As the woman wore gloves, the lettering was not decisive. Rosario could not recall if she had written the note with her left hand as the graphologist believed, a point that did not align with Iliescu's guilt as the Romanian was not left-handed.

The mossos had reviewed the tapes from the campus railway stations' security cameras, but they showed no woman or man who looked like the person described by the agent or like Iliescu who was now being upgraded from missing person to suspect. If the same person, as seemed evident, had carried out the crimes, Marcel Bru was not implicated. He was in the auditorium while Bellpuig was being killed; everyone had seen him. If the only lead was to Iliescu, the situation became complicated because they knew nothing of him other than what the Romanian police had told them. The consulate, for one, had never heard of him. When he arrived in Catalonia, he did not register there, but this was not strange as most Erasmus students failed to do so. Even though the Romanian consul couldn't provide any news about Iliescu, Manuela Vázquez insisted on meeting him.

Dimitri Vasilescu was used to speaking with the police and the sub-inspector's visit did not surprise him. As soon as he had arrived in Barcelona to take the helm at the consulate, he had to face a most uncomfortable situation: the admission that a number of associations such as the Catalan-Romanian Tanderei were fraudulent, as was the one in Badalona that one Cercel Gheorghe claimed to preside over. Gheorghe was a Romanian who had opened a bank account with false papers so good, unsuspecting folks could deposit money toward a sort of NGO to aid Romanians. These facts unnerved the consul to no end. He thought it most unfair that people in general made no reference to those "deeply honest immigrants in the face of missiles of mass destruction" and only paid attention to news that involved Romanians in criminal acts.

When he saw the sub-inspector, Vasilescu thought she'd come to ask for his cooperation in extraditing the parents of the underage girls who'd been stealing cell phones and hiding them in their vaginas. He blurted out to her about the issue, which the press had seized on after a tourist who had lost his phone, had grabbed the thieving minor and delivered her to a city cop patrolling down the Rambla.

The sub-inspector stopped him from going any further with the details as she realized that the consul was having a hard time. He was an older man, very proper from the old school. To speak to an unknown woman, even though she was from the police about underage vaginas used to smuggle cell phones must make him feel uneasy. Besides this, it couldn't be at all pleasant to keep receiving negative news about his compatriots. For this reason, before broaching the subject of Iliescu, Manuela started by praising some Romanian friends of hers, the Mateis – the consul might know them – and her optometrist who came from Timisoara and also the Romanian woman who had taken care with utmost devotion of her mother-in-law until her death. Dimitri Vasilescu was the person most interested in finding Iliescu. He had learned of his disappearance some fifteen days earlier; after Bru had alerted them, the mossos from the Sants station had informed the consul.

"Poor guy," the consul said, "I know he has no family…whoever made him disappear knows he won't be missed at home. He has no one to cry over his loss; in this respect, the girls are luckier."

And as a perplexed Manuela Vázquez stared at him, he asked her: "Don't you think so, madam?"

Manuela Vázquez smiled and tried to speak as kindly as possible.

"I think, consul, that Constantinu Iliescu is alive and I consider him a suspect, no matter how orphaned he might be, but on the last point, I do agree with you."

'My Lord!' Vasiliescu exclaimed, thinking that if the sub-inspector was telling the truth, he had better get ready to receive loads of abuse from the usual xenophobes who would again pelt his office with insults. "Do you have any proof?" he asked in a doleful voice and immediately, without waiting for an answer, added: "Tell me how I may help you."

Manuela Vázquez left his office with a list of all the Romanian associations in Barcelona and El Vallès that had registered with the consulate, as well as references to meeting places favored by Romanians and the names of two churches in which some Romanian priests watched for their far-from-home fellow citizens, just as Spanish priests had done with migrants working in Germany in the 1950s. They would have to see if they could find the lost needle in those haystacks.

The Romanian police kept looking for precedents in their country that might help them pull a thread of some usefulness, but they hadn't found any yet except for the license plate and the make and model of the white van, a Citroën Berlingo.

The Center for Criminal Investigation alerted the city police forces from Barcelona, Terrassa, Sabadell, Cerdanyola, Barberà del Vallès and Ciutat Badia, as well as taxi cooperatives and public parking garages to inform them immediately if they saw a van with those characteristics. Lluçanès requested that even if the vehicle's plates were not Romanian, they should ask for the driver's papers; Iliescu might have exchanged his plates for local ones in order to avoid detection.

The mossos working on the case, no longer referred to it as Cremona or Cremona-Arrigo, but as "Cremona–Arrigo–Bellpuig and a kite's tail," according to agent Cañizare who devoted extra-long hours to it. Lluçanès spurred them on from time to time to maintain morale and pointed the investigation toward Iliescu even though they would have to start from scratch. The few leads they had followed bore no results. The Italian police had decided that Dante Braccalente's hypothesis did not hold. Not all Neapolitans had to do with the mafia, nor could a link between the mob and Signora Cremona be established.

At the novelty stores in Barcelona and El Vallès – which agent Rifà had visited with utmost patience to show them a photograph of Iliescu and the composite portrait – no one recalled having sold toy cockroaches, flies or mice. But he got something from a mall in L'Illa – the tony Barcelona mall, a place the agent's sister had suggested because they sold amusing objects there such as key rings with wiggly animals, cloth mice that let out a whistle, flowers and penises that reacted to touch and the like. A salesgirl there told Rifà that on Tuesday, around 10 o'clock in the morning, when she had just opened, a young man, tall and husky, wearing a greasy cap and a dark jacket – she remembered having been startled by his dejected gaze – asked if they had a sort of plastic worm like the one in a photograph he showed her. As she said no, he asked her where he could find one or whether some manufacturer would agree to make one. The salesgirl agreed to make inquiries, but warned him that no one would accept the order unless it was for a good number of pieces. She had asked him how many worms he needed and he had answered, "All I need is one," She had then proposed to the young man some alternatives – centipedes, cockroaches, rats, mice, wasps – which he declined. "I have all these," he said politely. "This is the only one I need. I collect them."

"Before he left," the girl went on, "he asked for the shop's phone number; if he could not find his worm anywhere, he might risk putting in an order for a hundred. As he noted the number in a kind of appointment calendar, I noticed he was left-handed."

Rifà produced the composite portrait and Iliescu's photograph and showed them to her.

"Do you think it's him?"

The girl hesitated and finally said she didn't think they looked like her guy. The visitor's eyes were dark or so she thought and the one in the picture had light eyes. The composite portrait did not ring a bell at all.

Rifà called Lluçanès from the shop and hanging up, he addressed the salesgirl again: "If he should return, keep him here by any means and let us know right away. He is a dangerous criminal. What other salespersons are there here? May I speak with the manager?"

Even though the salesgirl had failed to identify her customer, Rifà felt quite pleased. Iliescu might have resorted to dark contacts and the cap had hidden his shaved head. If they found the murderer because of him, all his comrades would feel jealous and his friends in Polinyà where he was born and raised would congratulate him. And maybe with time, once he is made chief, they would name a street after him.

Lluçanès decided that the list of the Romanian gathering spots Manuela Vázquez had given him was useless. Everything pointed to Iliescu being a loner who did not relate with anyone. None of the other Erasmus scholars knew anything about him other than the girls and Bru, but Bru had confessed that in reality, he barely knew him and had decided to search for him in order to get closer to Laura. Despite believing he would get nowhere, Lluçanès mobilized his team and asked them to shed their uniforms. Dressed in civilian clothes, they were to drop by the Romanian spots with Iliescu's picture. The inspector had decided to examine Professor Bellpuig's life and began by interviewing his brother. He might take them to the mysterious Mònica, "his last victim." Unfortunately, August Bellpuig lived in Madrid and had no idea of Carles's extracurricular affairs.

37

The "Autònoma Assassin," as the media was calling him, had broken his typical pattern of attacking during the night between Friday and Saturday when he had killed Professor Bellpuig.

Friday was the holy day for Muslims, Agent Llobera had remarked. And too clever by half, he'd come close to telling the inspector that the perpetrator was an Islamist. But this supposition which he shared only with Cañizares – thus fortunately avoiding ridicule – made no sense. His colleague pointed out to him that it should be the other way round, that the day Muslims devoted to prayer and quiet did not fit the violence of the crimes and thus got them nowhere, particularly now that the murderer had chosen another day. If he were to strike again, he might kill on another Tuesday or perhaps that very Friday, 12th December.

Perhaps because it was Friday or because the reinforcements Lluçanès had requested had already arrived, the Bellaterra campus was teeming with mossos and security guards. Neither the police nor the academic authorities – now in true brotherhood, as the anti-Bologna pamphleteers had claimed they always were – were willing to tolerate a fourth crime.

With classes suspended because of the three days of mourning decreed by the rector after Bellpuig's death, the professors, if they chose to continue working at the Autònoma rather than at home, were instructed to lock themselves in their offices, instead of keeping their doors unlocked as they normally did.

Even the occupying students had decided to withdraw and as one of their *communiqués* put it, they weren't abandoning their sit-ins because they were afraid of the campus murderer or of the blows they could receive from the "pigs," but because their struggle had been distorted by the "miscommunication media" which were now attentive only to news related to the violent deaths. The authorities eager to sweep the democratic struggle of the anti-Bologna contingent under the rug might have been behind this. "In the capitalist system in which we live, the gruesome spectacles win the day and increase audience ratings to the highest levels," Miquel Oliver pontificated before a group of admirers. Due to this, he maintained, what had happened in Bellaterra played into their hands as it kept the public entertained, the people distracted and everyone forgetful that the School of Letters was occupied in the defense of student rights, in defense of freedom.

Little by little, the anti-Bologna contingent started to move out. Some began loading gas tanks, stoves, pots, pans, dishes and glasses into a van, while others folded sleeping bags, tied up mattresses and put blankets and clothes into bags to tote them away with greater ease. The last ones to leave on Friday afternoon were the leaders who aimed to fall in with the old maritime law (despite their landlubber looks) that dictated the captain should be the last one to abandon the ship.

On the rest of the campus, life went on, normal only in appearance; no one could forget the tragedy they had endured. The rector's team prepared their resignation for after the break and the forthcoming elections. Those cold, blustery days with low clouds, fog and rain weighed even heavier on the university community's spirits; they experienced their darkest hour. Many Erasmus scholars from the Vila had abandoned their apartments to return home. The brave ones who stayed put accepted gladly the reinforcements of the security guards. Besides the motorized patrols, there were agents standing near the gates of all the apartment buildings.

While the Vila was empty, the Hotel Serhs could barely cope with the sudden influx of guests. Foreign journalists, special envoys and TV crews occupied the rooms. They remained in Bellaterra awaiting developments and hoping to be the first to film the images of the next murder or perhaps interview the murderer himself.

38

On Friday, 12th December, the Italian consul finally managed to leave for the weekend with his girlfriend whom he had neglected for quite some time. He was exhausted and sad. The preceding Wednesday, the same day he had taken Signore Cremona-Hogarth to the airport with the remains of their daughter, he had welcomed Domenica's parents. Their head-to-toe mourning outfits and the deep sorrow they exuded gave them away to Braccalente. They did not need to spot the driver and the placard with their name. Fortunately, they remained in Barcelona just for the few hours needed to attend their daughter's cremation and then returned to Italy with an urn in their hands and their lives wrecked forever. The consul saw to all the bureaucratic paperwork and declared himself at their disposal. Domenica's mother said the only thing they needed was justice, to see the murderer pay with three death sentences for what he had done. Dante Braccalente did not dare contradict her or explain that the abolition of the death penalty had been an important democratic achievement in Spain; he could see things from their point of view. Had a daughter of his been killed, he would also call for the harshest punishment. Manuela Vázquez thought the same. She had gone with Lluçanès to see the Arrigos, thinking of her Sònia, but of course, did not mention her. She swore to them by the memory of Domenica (and in doing so, her voice broke), that they would arrest the murderer and bring him to justice.

Around six o' clock in the evening, while the Italian consul was in a suite of the Parador in Aiguablava, making love over a racket of squealing mattress coils and passionate panting, a cleaning squad contracted especially by the rector went into the Faculty of Letters. The occupiers had given up their posts barely one hour before, but the desire to erase all signs of their encampment as soon as possible with hygienic measures had led the acting dean – who was also the deputy dean of students – to request the cleaning operation as promptly as possible. About a dozen and a half workers divided the job by zones, following their manager's directions.

The area to the left was assigned to Juana and to Gladys and they moved toward one of the corridors that had been the preferred territory of the anti-Bologna pickets, a rather smelly spot. They must have used the classrooms as dormitories because the women found some abandoned sleeping bags there among empty cans, bottles and assorted garbage. The chairs and desks had been piled up helter-skelter in one corner.

Before addressing that disastrous battlefield of an encampment or an "encampusment," the women parked their war-machine: a cart with brooms, brushes, dusters, rags, mops, buckets, detergent, bleach, ammonia and other tools and products. Having placed the cart strategically and happy not to have to drag it any further, they took to inspecting the area while deciding first of all which would be the best approach to eliminate the stench in the air.

Juana proposed they start with the bathrooms. "The bitter pill first," she said resolutely. Surely that stink came from clogged toilets. A sign at the door warned they were out of order. But Gladys contradicted her: it didn't smell like shit, but like a skinned cat. She was sure of that. She knew what she was talking about, she said, and began to tell a gory story involving animal innards that the Santería folks of her native Dominican Republic used for voodoo rituals. Juana, a Catalan from Ripollet, was mesmerized.

As they opened a door, a putrid and somewhat sweet, unbearable odor made them take a step back.

"I told you," Gladys insisted to her companion, "there's got to be a dead animal here."

Then Juana, who belonged to the union, mentioned that their contract made no reference to having to clean up after dead flesh, and the two of them decided to look for their supervisor so he could figure out who was supposed to take care of this mess or he himself could deal with it. Didn't they say that he earned a good salary?

Joan López, the head of the cleaning team, had no desire to argue with Juana about the contract or listen to the blather Gladys was spewing about rituals involving dead animals. He didn't tell them what he thought either: that they were a pair of milksops, like all women, besides belonging to the party of "work be gone, rest don't leave me" and decided to go there and see for himself where the smell came from.

Holding his nose with his left hand – it really stank – Joan López opened the toilet doors one after the other. He began by the women's: they were clogged, but there was nothing to prevent those lazy bums from cleaning them. Then he went to the men's. There he felt like running back, but if he left, he would be agreeing with the women. With an effort to breathe only through the mouth and keep his nostrils blocked, he kicked the only door there was, after the row of urinals, where the stench came from. As the door opened he saw right away what produced the foul smell: sitting on the toilet, with his pants and briefs down, there was a man with his skull broken, his eyes wide open, his face and body splotched with dried blood. There was a belt tied around his neck. Lying on the floor, broken, were his eyeglasses.

39

It didn't take long for the mossos patrolling the campus to cordon off the area and call Lluçanès. The inspector and the forensics team arrived at the same time. Just like the cleaning women one hour before, they were also pushing a cart with the tools that would make their task easier, among them, some face masks to protect them from the emanations of death.

Judging from the condition of the body, the inspector surmised it must have been decomposing for three or four days in that humiliating posture. The murderer might have caught him while he was obeying nature's call or he might have forced him to lower his pants and underwear and sit on the toilet before striking his head with a blunt object, a hammer or wrench, which had fractured open his skull and revealed his brain.

Whoever had done it had followed the same method as with Professor Bellpuig and probably on the same day. The corpse had not been found before possibly because it lay in occupier's territory where no one went other than the anti-Bologna contingent, and that bunch had confirmed that the toilets were out of order as the sign on the premises declared. Lluçanès favored this version over one that would have him suppose that the occupiers knew there was a dead body nearby and that their hatred of the mossos prevented them from calling the police. The sign, handwritten in capital letters, had been placed inside a plastic bag just in case it could be a clue. Could the murderer have written it? And could he have done so wearing gloves? Or did he push his victim inside precisely because those toilets were out of order?

The dead man's face was quite disfigured. "Who could it be?" the inspector asked himself. It was probably a student, but it could also be a professor or a staff member or any person not related to the university who had gone there with the anti-Bologna pickets. Lluçanès drew his cell phone from his pocket and called Manuela Vázquez to give her the news and ask her to drop by as soon as she could. During those trying days, the inspector had come to appreciate her. At first, he didn't like her. He thought she boasted too often about her talent as a psychologist and her college degree. He had only studied at the police academy and was contemptuous about assets that came from any source other than the Mossos d'Esquadra. But now he saw that his first impression had been wrong. Manuela Vázquez was an excellent coworker with an extraordinary capacity for work, and his team respected her a lot. But all that had not been of much use; her candidates for murderer had all turned out to be innocent. And now, when it came to finding out if the murderer was Iliescu, she could not offer any other proof besides some coincidence between similarities in his photograph and the police sketch of a person who was far from being proven as involved in the crimes. The rest were suppositions that could have been made by any reader of detective fiction: Iliescu had disappeared to make people believe he was far away and thus be able to attack without arousing suspicion. He acted with great cool, methodically, using disguises and besides writing a note in a false hand was capable of faking a throat ailment so as not to be betrayed by his voice. But Manuela forgot one important detail: Iliescu did not use his left hand as the murderer was believed to do.

The sub-inspector did not take long to arrive. Her office in the Cerdanyola station was a ten-minute drive from the School of Letters. She felt as upset and disgusted as her superior, if not more. Where was that serial murderer headed? Why did he humiliate and mock them in such an unbearable manner? Who would the next victim be?

The face of the young man, even though it was disfigured, reminded her of Bru and his small, rather scrawny body matched that of the student. Besides, the frame of the glasses he wore was the same as Bru's. She was sure of that. She always noticed people's glasses, perhaps because she had such a hard time choosing ones for herself that would not make her look ungainly. But until they checked his fingerprints or until his family could identify him, she could not be absolutely certain that it was Bru.

The belt around the neck had left a purple mark. Lluçanès and Vázquez looked everywhere for the murderer's signature, but found nothing. It was natural to assume that the same person had killed the girls and the professor, but this time there was no plastic bug placed anywhere, at least not that the police could see.

"He might have placed it somewhere else, in a pocket or perhaps in his rectum," the sub-inspector said, recalling the location of the plastic mouse in the first murder. The inspector hadn't thought of it and imagined it was a strong possibility.

It had been a good while since the forensic team had finished their work when the examiner and the judge arrived. They were late due to an accident slowing highway traffic. They were both taken aback by the brutality of the murderer's act and looked at Lluçanès in silent reproach. How was it possible that he hadn't caught that dangerous psychopath yet? What were the police waiting for? The inspector, as though accepting the silent rebuke, spoke out loud quite sincerely: "The worst thing is that we do not know where he's hiding or how to catch him. This time he might have left a clue to help with things."

Then he addressed the examiner and asked him to start the autopsy as soon as possible. His own wife might threaten divorce because of neglect – he hadn't been home since taking over the case – but he wanted to be present in the autopsy room. Afraid of getting sick, Manuela Vázquez excused herself. The inspector asked her to call Bru's family and send them to the Forensic Anatomical Institute. Manuela Vázquez swallowed hard. She hated the task. Bru was an only child. She didn't even dare think of the parents' desolation.

Back in her office where she planned to make the call, she speed-dialed 1 on her personal cell phone. She needed to hear her daughter's voice. She didn't tell her the reason each time, but ever since they had begun finding the bodies at the Autònoma, she had insisted on hearing from her. Sònia had her cell off or out of range and it didn't accept messages. The sub-inspector became even more nervous and was mad at herself: what relationship could there be between Sònia and the murderer? None, to be sure. This was just a neurotic overreaction.

Before calling Bru's parents, Manuela Vázquez contacted Rosario Hurtado. The agent had a free weekend, much deserved since she'd been working her butt off, but she was ready to go back to work whenever Manuela desired.

"You know, Sub-Inspector, that I want a destination closer to my home," she had told her that very Friday before leaving, "and I need points in my favor. Antoni has insisted that once we're married I work at a nearer station, so it doesn't take me two hours to get to and from work. I mean, I should have a little more time to be with him. This afternoon, as soon as Antoni is done with his medical practice, we are going to look for an apartment."

Manuela Vázquez felt bad thwarting the real-estate plans of her colleague and her fiancé, a young doctor who had just got a job with the Social Security to work in Gavà, near Castelldefels where they lived, but the sub-inspector thought the agent's help was necessary and asked her to come back to work. She was the one who had dealt most with Marcel Bru and she was the perfect person to contact his roommates as soon as Lluçanès gave the go-ahead. Then she again called her daughter. She couldn't reach her this time either. Finally, she called Marcel Bru's parents.

"This is Sub-Inspector Manuela Vázquez," she said.

"We don't want to talk to the police," a woman's voice answered in an aggressive tone before hanging up.

Manuela Vázquez tried again up to a half dozen times; they had left the phone off the hook. Then she contacted Lluçanès and breathed easier when he told her he'd make sure to send someone from the team to get the parents. In the meantime, she could start looking at the files of the picketers and decide if it was advisable to interrogate someone. Some of the protesters had been active in the Bellaterra occupation; they would have to speak with them. If Bru's body had been there all those days, it was highly unlikely that no one had noticed.

Vázquez received a call from Lluçanès around 9 o'clock at night. He ordered her to go home and get as much rest as possible because the following day, Saturday, they would have to go to work. The dead man was indeed, Marcel Bru.

40

When Lluçanès met his team on Saturday morning, he began his sermon – as Rosario Hurtado referred to his addresses – with the wish that it would turn out to be the last weekend he would have to ask them to work. They all deserved a rest he told them, but the only way to get one was finding the murderer and that's why he was urging them to put all their energy into their work, to spare no effort and so on and so forth. He continued unloading sacks of goodwill for a while, pacing up and down the room.

The inspector's tone of voice showed his annoyance. Ten minutes earlier, the director general of the Department of the Interior had scolded him on the phone, stressing that it was inadmissible that a criminal held Catalan society in fear and that he had to be arrested immediately.

"Can't you see that we'll be forced to resign if you can't find him?," the director general had concluded despondently.

Those words made the inspector realize what was getting the politician's goat and he answered that he appreciated the plural, but that no one would call for his own resignation because his was not a position, but a rank. And as for the cooperation offered to find the murderer, it was true he needed reinforcements to scrutinize the parking lots in the towns of El Vallès and the residential developments close to Bellaterra.

Putting up with the threats of that fool so early in the morning was the last thing he needed after having had an argument with his wife who resented the fact that he hadn't come home a single day at a decent hour or been able to see his children when they were awake for almost two weeks since that debacle had started. He had seen them only at breakfast at 7 o' clock in the mornings and had to leave without driving them to school as he normally would do. Marga did not understand how bad things were for him. Only Pura, his secretary, seemed to understand him. Better not to think of her now; he had enough with the difficult case and felt impotent and frustrated, but he needed to avoid letting people see it at all costs. Never show weakness. On the contrary, he had to appear resolute and strong. He must convert his bad mood into energy and spread it to his coworkers. He tried. He cut his initial sermon short which everybody was thankful for and gave them the information advanced by the examiner, even though his report was not yet typed.

The autopsy revealed that Marcel Bru had died on Tuesday 9th around three o' clock in the afternoon, just about three hours after Bellpuig. It was likely that the guy had been answering nature's call without latching the door to the toilet which had not been forced open as they had verified yesterday. What seemed clear, according to the examiner, was that he had not been dragged there after he died; there were no marks indicating that. He must have been caught by surprise, seated on the toilet. In that position, it was easy for the intruder to break his head. It was simply a matter of delivering a blunt blow, the same as the murderer had done to Bellpuig. Before leaving, however, the perpetrator had resorted to strangling again.

Bru was not wearing a tie, and although at first the forensic team thought the murderer had used his victim's belt, they later ascertained it wasn't his or even his size, but a new belt from an expensive brand: Lotusse, three or four sizes larger. It was probably used for the first time and it would have been bought for the occasion. Senora Bru had also told them that her son never wore a belt. He hated belts, "as he hated everything that oppresses people," the woman uttered amid sobs. Since she was crying for the death of a son, Lluçanès restrained himself from telling her that the argument that belts oppress people was poor

Marcel's mistaken rationalization, which took people's butts for their temples.

"The brand of the belt could tell us about the tastes of the murderer, sir," Llobera interrupted, raising his hand to request permission to speak as they normally did at meetings.

"Or perhaps he used an expensive brand to be nice to his victim," the sub-inspector muttered sarcastically. "We might discover he's a man with exquisite tastes."

"He can't be," Rosario blurted out, "he wouldn't be leaving plastic bugs around if he were."

"Quiet!" Lluçanès shouted, "and let's focus on the essentials. The belt would be useful only if it brought us some new clue and right now..."

"What about fingerprints? Are there fingerprints?" It was again Llobera asking. He was ruffled because he thought they had not taken his supposition seriously.

The belt had been handled with gloves, just as had the murder weapon which this time had been found. Lluçanès explained to them that the night before Corporal Lluc had been scouring the toilet tanks as he had a premonition that the murderer could have disposed of the weapon there. He found it actually, not in the spot he suspected, but in a closet separated from the stall where they had found the body by a wall that did not reach the ceiling. One of the janitors had a key and let him in. The murderer had discarded the weapon – a medium-size hammer with quite a sharp peen and blunt face – tossing it through the opening between the stall and the janitor's closet. The inspector congratulated the corporal in the presence of his companions for the discovery.

A happy Lluc thanked him. He wanted to climb the merits ladder and like all young people, do it fast.

No one was surprised to find out that the perpetrator planned things carefully. The belt was further proof of that and led them to a simple deduction which Rosario Hurtado spelled out: "The murderer must have known Bru. If he took the precaution of purchasing a belt, it was because he knew

Bru would not wear one. It seems his pants were always about to fall down."

"Which means," Rifà said, "that he is an observant friend or companion."

"I agree that he is observant," the sub-inspector joined in. "Iliescu fits the profile to a tee, but not to the point of 'presenting'," she made the quotation marks gesture, "Bru with a belt because he thought his pants would fall to the floor."

"People think that to commit a murder you need a gun or at least a jack knife or a sharp kitchen knife," ventured Llobera again, "and they don't realize that it's easy to kill someone; all you need is a good object or tool you can find in any house ... Or you can even kill with a rock."

"Of course," Lluçanès said in a tone that underscored the obvious statement he'd just heard. Llobera was having a most astute day. "There are varied ways to murder someone, but luckily murderers represent a small percentage, at least in our country. Let's get to work. The other point I wanted to share with you all is that this time the little beast is not made of plastic but of paper – a picture copied on paper from the Web that the murderer placed in Bru's pants pocket."

"This identifies him as the person who went to the mall at L'Illa, looking for the worm and as he couldn't find one ..." This time it was Rifà who spoke.

The inspector resumed his talk: "We know he's tall and strong and seems to be a leftie from the way he attacked with the hammer according to the examiner and from this, in effect, we can deduce that it's the same person mentioned by the salesgirl."

"But, where is he? And why does he kill?" the sub-inspector asked. "What's he trying to tell us? And what is the sense of the little creatures he leaves behind? Can you show us the paper with the worm?" she asked Lluçanès.

"It's still at the lab. If you want, I can ask them to bring it up."

"I'll go down myself, if you don't mind and have a good look. Do we know from what Web site he got it?"

"They are trying to find out. They'll let us know."

The sub-inspector did not take long to return. When she came in, she asked Lluçanès's permission to check Bellpuig's laptop. She had thought the photocopy came from a picture she had seen on the professor's screen on the day of his death.

41

They switched on Bellpuig's computer and saw a picture of some peaches on the screen. It was a still life, which the sub-inspector had seen before on that very screen splashed with blood when she had gone into the professor's office. A black worm threaded its way among the peaches. It was the same bug that appeared in the copy found in Bru's pocket, the same one the murderer had used after downloading the picture from some museum's Web site. She had no doubt. She searched the computer to see if she could find other pictures. On the desk there was a folder with the inscription "ERASMUS CLASSES." Manuela Vázquez opened it. She found a flash drive with the PowerPoint Bellpuig had used for what must have been one of his last lectures because it was dated 5th November, just before the pickets had prevented access to the classrooms; it had also served as the departing point for an assignment. The question for this appeared in a document titled "'Life Almost Still': What points in common and what differences can you find among these pictures?" It showed four well-known still lifes by Zurbarán – *Still Life with Quince, Still Life with Pots and Pans, Basket with Oranges* and *Breakfast with Chocolate* – and four pictures by a painter, Flegel, she had not heard of: *Still Life with Dessert, Still Life with Cockroach, Still Life with Fish* and *Peaches*. She looked at them carefully. The first one, next to a platter with nuts and dried fruit, showed a disgusting mouse. In the second, an enormous beetle made its way across a tablecloth with dishes and food. On the third, a revolting fly sat on a loaf of bread. The mouse, the cockroach, the fly...those were the creatures that had been placed on the bodies of the victims, just as the black worm. Manuela Vázquez leapt off her chair and got her cell from her pocket.

"Inspector Lluçanès," she cried, "I think I've got it! I think the objects have to do with paintings, and the paintings are by a painter whose work Bellpuig showed to his class."

"Manuela, I don't understand," Lluçanès replied, "what paintings are you talking about?"

"The disgusting little critters have to do with paintings," she reiterated. "Can you show me the folder with the exam papers that you got from Bellpuig's office?"

"Of course. What do you want to see? The graphology experts brought it back. My secretary keeps it in her files. I'll tell her to bring it over."

Lluçanès secretary was a good-looking woman who was always made-up and dressed to kill. Some thought that her stockings and miniskirts were inappropriate for her job. Others, however, appreciated them. Besides, if Lluçanès thought it was OK, who were they to object? Lluçanès looked at his secretary as though he liked what he saw, perhaps because her looks contrasted pleasantly with his wife's. In the photo on his desk, his wife, wearing a shirtdress down to her shins, looked like a novice about to become a nun. Pura, whose name did not fit the lust she inspired, soon came in with the file.

Manuela Vázquez read Iliescu's exam paper carefully. His small hand, pointy and nervous had been analyzed by the graphologists, but no attention had been paid to its content. Attentive only to the traits of the writing, they probably had missed what the one signed by Iliescu said: "With the insects and disgusting vermin – a rat, a cockroach, a fly and a worm – the painter might have wanted to introduce a disquieting element, he wanted to tell us we must beware. In a certain way, Flegel is trying to say the same as the classic adage: *latet anguis in herba* – 'a snake lies in the grass.' This counterpoint between life and death is absent in Zurbarán, even though Eros and Thanatos normally walk hand in hand. Zurbarán's still lifes make no mention of that, at least those I've been able to see. I've read that Flegel's painting may be considered a predecessor of the *vanitates*, those pictures which, to remind us of our mortality, feature a skull."

A nervous and excited Manuela Vázquez showed the inspector what she had found. They could have no doubt now of Iliescu's guilt: the relationship between the macabre symbols left on the victims' bodies and the revolting creatures that appeared in Flegel's paintings was obvious. Fortunately, Iliescu had mentioned only four of those. Did this mean there would be no further crimes? And why had he chosen the people he had killed? Perhaps Laura herself, before dying, told him she had made love with Bru or Iliescu had imagined it when he went to meet her when Bru dropped her off in Bellaterra the night of Friday the 28th after watching the program where she spoke of his disappearance. But how did he manage to find out that Bellpuig and Domenica had been together? Did he see them when he waited for Laura from his hiding place as they went to the apartment? Had he that night got into the apartment without the student or the professor noticing? He might even have a copy of the key…If he was to move in with the girls, it stood to reason that Laura would have given him one.

The sub-inspector was quite an intuitive person, but intuition cuts both ways, because it could lead one up the wrong path, a path she thought was right, unlike before with Bru and Bellpuig. "If we had examined the essay ourselves instead of the graphologists," she lamented, "we might at least have prevented Bru's murder."

"Let us not torment ourselves," said the inspector. "We've done all we could; it wasn't our job to compare handwriting. I also believe he will not kill again. We need to catch him, Manuela, but let me confess that I don't think we will. He is too smart, he uses disguises, he pulls our legs…If we weren't honest people, we could blame the crazy bum who attacked Rosario, as they say they did in the US with the Gainesville campus murderer. They accused a homeless vagabond in order to return calm to the university which, like ours, was in the clutches of horror."

"But we cannot do that, Inspector," Manuela said with conviction, "even if we are becoming more and more like the Americans."

"That wasn't really my press conferences, however."

"We do have leads, but we do not know if they'll help us arrest Iliescu." said Manuela.

42

The afternoon of that same Saturday, a number of agents of the Mossos d'Esquadra visited gas stations in the areas of El Vallès, Barcelona and Girona. They carried photographs of Iliescu and offering some reward money as a lure, asked the employees for an identification or for any clue that could help locate the missing man.

That same afternoon, the sub-inspector once again called Rosa Casasaies to get the addresses and phone numbers of all the student protesters who had locked themselves into the School of Letters. Their testimonials could be valuable regarding Marcel Bru's death. Obtaining the data wouldn't be easy since the students came from different schools and departments which would necessitate an extraordinary meeting with professors from a number of units. They would have to wait until Monday.

On Monday, once the university opened, everything would be easier and also more complicated. They would have to suspend classes in mourning for the new death. With the dean still on leave – she had been admitted to the hospital with a severe case of anxiety – it the responsibility fell on the associate dean of students to organize a memorial for Marcel Bru. Luckily, Rosa Casasaies would not have to participate. Bru was neither an Erasmus student nor had he enrolled in any of her classes. She would attend because she felt she should, like the rest of the faculty, but would not have to speak. In her state of nervous tension, she would not have been up to it.

Inspector Lluçanès had been called to a meeting early in the afternoon with the ministers of the Interior and of universities and also with the rector to brief them on the conclusions he had reached, thanks mainly to Manuela Vázquez. At this point, neither he nor any member of his team had any doubts: left or right-handed, the murderer was an Erasmus student; they knew his name and supposed he had faked a disappearance as an alibi. He was a very smart psychopath who, he was sure, had not chosen his victims at random, but because they were somehow related to one another – a relationship he deemed objectionable and felt obliged to punish them for it. He probably fit the type called "apostolic," one who felt it is his calling to carry out the sacred mission of cleansing filth and eliminating all he considered evil or wrong.

Keeping Bru's name a secret prevented the spread of new conclusions. The media would have a field day if they learned about it and the universities competing with the Autònoma would have died of delight; they might well have resorted to the negative publicity in vogue these days which stressed the failings of others over one's own accomplishments.

The about-to-resign rector felt depressed and humiliated for having to make *Autònoma* history as the 'Rector of the Murders' after a rather brilliant career there. He insisted that everyone should keep mum about the victims' sexual relationships because he foresaw a public statement being mocked: "For us, the moral standing of university life is paramount. Our university guarantees it, unlike what happens on other campuses."

The rivalry to attract students, so fierce lately, must have its limits, he told them. The time was ripe to request a kind of ethics code from the minister that would make all Catalan universities value scientific merits exclusively, an area in which the Autònoma excelled and stop blaming it for the bad luck of having had an occupation or having been chosen by a madman to kill three students and a professor. The minister of the interior said he would look into it, although he wasn't particularly concerned about what would happen at the Autònoma. He was much more interested in other universities with a management ideologically closer to the party that had given him his position and hoped to pressure the government so that the new rector came from the same party or at least, was more friendly to it than the present one with whom he had never seen eye to eye. To him, the rector's resignation was welcome news. He might even celebrate it with his team and see to it that a professor with the same militancy presented himself for election.

The minister who had declared warm feelings for the anti-Bologna occupiers, expressed a need to open a nation-wide debate "to discuss the role of the university, which might have become an obsolete institution, no longer necessary at the present time." Right at that moment, Lluçanès's phone rang.

"Inspector, we have a patrol following a white Citroën Berlingo on the AP-7 motorway toward Barcelona. Its license plate is the same as Iliescu's."

"I'm sorry," Lluçanès told the ministers as he got up, "I have to rush off. It seems that some agents have located Iliescu's vehicle and we can't let him get away." He left the room, leaving the rector and the interior minister at each other's throats.

43

Two nearby mossos mobile patrol units joined the vehicle that had detected the van on National Highway 156 near Cassà de la Selva and had followed it as it veered into motorway AP-7 to Barcelona. Following Lluçanès strict orders, none of them had turned on their sirens or the blue flashing lights. The inspector left in a hurry for the Egara Complex to coordinate the operation and hopped onto a helicopter which flew toward the motorway. They soon spotted the van that, in fact, matched Iliescu's model. The inspector issued his orders from the air: "Be alert and don't lose him. Let one of the cars get in front of him and the other two behind. Intercept him at the first toll. Got it? Got it?"

"Yes, sir."

"Got it, sir."

"Sir, this is Corporal Beltran and Agent Margarida Pou. We were patrolling near the Cassà airport when we spotted him. Both the model and plate were the ones we've been searching for! We turned around to follow him. We suspect he was coming from the airport.'

"Good job, Corporal. Stay on task and follow my orders. Have you seen his face?"

"No, sir, but as he is going fairly slowly, never over a hundred kilometers, we'll overtake him and look."

"Very well. Remember his picture. Blue eyes, shaven head, a prominent nose. Of course, he could be in disguise, even as a woman."

"Thank you, sir."

"To all patrols: this is Inspector Lluçanès. We are flying over the Lloret-Sant Feliu area and have the suspect's car in sight. We are flying high so as not to get his attention; if he sees the chopper, he might get off the motorway and that's not good. We'll arrest him when he stops at the toll. OK?"

"Yes, sir," responded all three patrols.

Lluçanès thought the least dangerous way to catch Iliescu was to intercept him when he'd stop at the motorway's toll barrier. Even though the murderer had never used a gun to kill, he might be armed and the inspector did not want his men to run unnecessary risks, much less innocent drivers who could happen to be on the motorway at that unpropitious moment.

All the mossos taking part in the operation felt at once uneasy and excited, bursting with adrenaline. For some of them, this was the first dangerous mission in which they were involved, a fact that made them feel like the policemen in films. Normally, their work was rather humdrum and boring: jotting down statements from petty thieves, responding to accusations, getting suspicious-looking people to show their papers and the like. They seldom rose to occasions like the present one, which was like those they had dreamed about when entering the police academy.

From the helicopter, Lluçanès radioed an alert to all the patrols near that stretch of toll way and called Granollers for reinforcements in case Iliescu decided to take that direction and could not be intercepted. He then connected with his team and sent Corporal Lluc and Agent Cañizares toward the motorway. He wanted them to wait on the other side of the tollgate at Cardedeu-la Roca.

Lluc and Cañizares were in Barcelona in the Raval district; they had just interviewed the priest of an aid center for Romanians and needed to make their way posthaste. At that hour, the Littoral Beltway, the most direct route to get to the Girona motorway from their location in Barcelona, had heavy traffic. Lluc turned on the siren and lights to weave their way through it and pressed the gas pedal. If they had really found the Autònoma's murderer, they didn't want to miss the moment of his arrest. Nor did the inspector. He would witness it from the air, even though he would have preferred to coordinate the operation from the ground and catch Iliescu himself. He regretted not having Manuela by his side to enjoy the arrest directly and called her.

"Sub-Inspector," he said to her, "we are in pursuit of Iliescu's van. Light a candle to a saint of your devotion and get the toll company on the phone. You know the license plate number, right? Ask them not to raise their barrier if he decides to take the manual payment lane." With this request, he was making her part of the action.

"I'm on it and let me know as soon as he is in handcuffs."

"Count on it."

"Be careful," the sub-inspector added in a motherly way.

On the helicopter's radio, he heard Lluc's voice cursing Iliescu and his entire ilk.

"Inspector, this is Corporal Lluc and Agent Cañizares. We are approaching the Trinitat ramp on the Littoral Beltway. We are going as fast as we can. We want to get to the point of encounter as soon as possible. He won't get through, no way."

The inspector addressed all the patrols: "He is turning toward the service area by Sant Celoni. Patrols 1 and 2. Ready?"

The two cars following the van also veered into the service area. In Agent Cañizares's opinion, Iliescu could want to refuel or have a cup of coffee, but when he realized he was being followed, he could try to lose them or set a trap.

"What if he's carrying explosives?" he asked the corporal.

"No, man, it doesn't fit the profile," Lluc answered. "He's just trying to prove he can take us for a ride. Or perhaps he wants us to arrest him at last; it wouldn't be the first time something like that happened. A thirst for notoriety makes them do it."

"You may be right. That's why it's not surprising that he hasn't put false plates on his van."

They went quiet as they heard the inspector's voice again.

"As soon as he gets out, you've got to stop him and shackle him."

"What I would give to handcuff him!" Cañizares exclaimed. "Laura and Domenica were beautiful! Son of a bitch, bastard, go rot in prison, you motherfucker."

A grating sound from the receiver made them stop talking. Again they heard Lluçanès's voice: "He didn't get out of the car. He might have noticed we've been following him. He went through the gas station lane without stopping. Lluc, go toward the Montcada service area."

"Yes, sir."

They were on the ramp to the Girona motorway; they had to go up, turn around and go down to wait for Iliescu. Their Seat Toledo was humming. The corporal loved speed. He never missed a race and would have liked to become a race driver. It took them less than five minutes. They got there and parked on a shoulder from which they could control Iliescu's arrival perfectly. Lluc had to roll down the window because the tobacco smoke bothered him. Cañizares had lit a cigarette. He was so nervous that he had to either smoke or bite his nails which the corporal could not stand.

"I hope they let us know if they catch him at the toll. We don't want to be kept waiting," Lluc said.

"We'll get a break as soon as he's in jail. You know? I met a hot girl at the Romanian bar in Mollet," Cañizares told him. "She could not give me any leads for Iliescu, she'd never seen him, but we have a date for Sunday. Her name is Irina. She was born in a little town in the Carpathians."

"Be careful. She could be a relative of Count Dracula. I would have preferred to go to the toll. They'll catch him there and we'll miss it."

Again they heard the inspector's voice. He sounded angry.

"I just got a call from Sabadell connecting me with Mònica Terribas, the newswoman. One of you will have to pay for having informed TV3; I'll sure as hell open proceedings. She's sent a mobile team over. She wants to televise Iliescu's detention. We can't allow that. We better stop him right away and avoid the cameras. Get right behind him and intercept, OK?"

The helicopter planed over the motorway and as close to the ground as it could, making a horrifying racket. By chance, the traffic was smooth and it was easy to intercept Iliescu. Corporal Beltran ordered the suspect to get out of the van: "Constantinu Iliescu, get out with your hands in the air."

44

Iliescu obeyed, showing no resistance and only when he saw they were about to put handcuffs on him did he ask why he was being detained. He was sure, he added, that at no time he had driven over the speed limit, 120 km per hour, and he'd gone even much more slowly because he had little gas left and wanted it to last until he reached Barcelona.

"Don't give us this bullshit," Corporal Beltran spat at him. "You know quite well why we are arresting you, you filthy murderer. For the killing of four people, don't you think that's enough?"

"You must be confused," Iliescu retorted determinedly, watching in awe the spread of mossos around him. 'I've done nothing." But seeing that it was useless to flee or oppose them, he let them shackle his hands to his back.

During the whole ride to the Sabadell station, he kept insisting on his innocence and swore he hadn't killed anyone, but the mossos told him to shut up and that as soon as they got to Sabadell he would have a lawyer for his defense and he'd be allowed one phone call.

"Call the Romanian consulate," he said. "I want the consul to know and I hope he'll send me a lawyer."

A shaken Dimitri Vasilescu responded to the call from the presumed Autònoma assassin, as everybody called him. When he heard Iliescu reiterate his innocence, insisting he didn't know why he was there, the consul believed him. For the sake of the good name of Romanians, it better be a mistake on the part of the police and Iliescu, despite what the police thought, innocent. He rushed to Sabadell with a lawyer friend of his whom he trusted.

Maties Martorell specialized in the defense of immigrants. He was a member of a well-known family of lawyers from Vic, but had decided to practice in Barcelona instead and with a colleague who was to become his wife, had opened an office for helping those who, despite having the law on their side, were victimized by people in positions of power. By helping Romanians who had been illegally fired or defrauded by unscrupulous people, he had met Dimitri Vasilescu and they had become friends to the point that the consul was now the godfather of Dimitri Martorell i Castellarnau, the third child of the lawyer couple.

The consul couldn't have found a better person to defend his countryman. Apart from the kindness Maties showed to Romanians, he was learning their language. In Iliescu's case, however, he did not need to use his linguistic knowledge because he realized at once that the student's Catalan was much better than his own Romanian.

Iliescu asked the lawyer why he had been arrested. He couldn't see the logic in the fleet of cars that intercepted him on the motorway as if he were an international criminal, a mafia thug wanted for a number of crimes committed in different countries or cast as an extra in an action movie. When Maties Martorell informed him he was being accused of the death of three of his friends from the university and one professor, Iliescu was stunned. He swore time and again that he had nothing to do with it, that he was incapable of hurting a fly, that he detested violence. He admitted he had a brief relationship with Laura Cremona and knew her friend Domenica Arrigo and also Marcel Bru and admired Professor Bellpuig. The few of his classes he had attended – there hadn't been many and some of them had been taught by the assistant – had interested him a lot. He wanted to study art and since the pickets prevented the course's development, had decided to hop on a bus and go to Madrid to visit the Prado as recommended by Bellpuig and look for a painting by Pieter van Steenwyck instead of moving in with Laura and Domenica as he had previously planned. He had alerted Laura that he wouldn't show up, but hadn't told her the truth. He hadn't even thought of going back to Romania. He had sent her an e-mail, not bothering to phone. He was weary of Laura, he admitted; her stalking annoyed him. He was used to being alone, had always lived by himself and besides, Laura's promiscuity displeased him. He didn't think it was right. At the last minute, he had decided he would not go live with her and her friend and instead he go away for a week. Once back, he'd make a decision, but when he returned from Madrid he happened to see Laura on television, claiming that he had disappeared; she was holding his picture and saying they had posted it all over the university, the metro stations and the Gràcia neighborhood, where he lived. The whole thing revolted him. Why on earth had she appointed herself his keeper? Why were they looking for him if he had left on his own volition? It was then that he decided to go far away, to be left alone so Laura would not look for or pester him. If he hadn't been quite sure he wanted to live with her, now he had no doubt. To get out of Barcelona, he spoke to a friend who lived in London from the cybercafé near his place in Nou Barris and asked if he could spend a few days at his house. The friend told him he'd be welcome and Iliescu searched the Web for a cheap flight. He bought a ticket for an early morning flight next day with Ryanair from Girona and drove his van to the Girona airport where he parked the car until his return. Now it was only some four hours, five at most, since he'd come back from London; he couldn't be quite sure. With all the confusion, he had lost count of time.

"If what you say is true, if you can prove it, it will not be hard to prove you innocent," Maties Martorell told him, patting him on the shoulder. "Do you recall at what time the flight for London departed?"

"Yes, I do. I got up really, really early. I left my place at about four o' clock in the morning because the airplane was departing at six o' clock and I had to be at the airport at least one hour earlier."

"Laura was killed between four and five o' clock that morning," the lawyer told him, looking into his eyes. "You could have driven to Bellaterra and then to Girona. I would prefer you told us the truth…didn't you think of killing her? You yourself said you felt ambushed by her. I will be better able to help you if you don't lie."

"I have no intention of lying. I didn't kill Laura, I assure you. I didn't do it, I swear. From home I went straight to the motorway. I keep everything. I'm a pack rat and have copies of the receipts from the tolls and of my boarding pass. I suppose those should be proof enough."

"Where do you keep that?"

"In my bag at the back of the van, unless someone has taken it so they can charge me with the murders."

45

The police examined the travel bag Iliescu said he kept in the back of his van with painstaking zeal. It produced a folder with some documents: the receipt for the toll, stamped at 4:45 a.m. on Saturday, 29th November at the exit booth of motorway AP-7 for the Girona airport and a copy of the Ryanair boarding pass for that same day at 6:05 a.m. to fly to London's Luton airport. His lawyer affirmed that those documents proved Iliescu's innocence, yet Lluçanès didn't think they were conclusive enough: Iliescu could have killed Laura in time to get to the Girona airport and catch the flight. As for the other crimes, he would have to prove he was out of the country at the time and had not returned to move Laura's body from his van to the crevice where it had been found and carry out the other murders as though he were some sort of Abaddon, the exterminating angel, who wanted to cleanse the world and mete out punishment and justice. After his arrest, all the mossos who had collaborated in the operation were sure of his guilt, mainly because they accepted Sub-Inspector Manuela Vázquez's conclusions, as she had explained them to the team during an emergency gathering at the Egara Complex: "I suppose," the sub-inspector had said, "that seeing his picture on TV was the last straw and angry, he went to Bellaterra. He might have called her before to tell her he'd returned. We do not know because Laura's cell phone has not been found. Or maybe not; he might have waited for her sitting on the stairs until the fateful moment or he could have had the key to her apartment. He went in and saw Domenica who claimed she loved Marcel Bru, screwing Professor Bellpuig. That image was deeply disagreeable. He decided to punish them. He was exacting vengeance against promiscuity."

"Then, Sub-Inspector, you believe that the clash between our promiscuity and his values was the detonator that led him to kill?" Rosario Hurtado asked.

"*Our* sexual promiscuity," Lluçanès echoed her mockingly, "I'm not following, Agent. Are you all promiscuous?"

The group laughed, Rosario turned red and corrected herself.

"I was speaking in general about our society, the young..."

The sub-inspector came to her defense: "Statistics show that 60 percent of young people are sexually promiscuous. In this sense, the sexual habits of advanced industrialized societies have changed a lot. My generation and even yours, Inspector, understood sex differently. There was strong religious pressure and also male domination, much more than today. The fact that a man could end up with a child that wasn't his set a high value on virginity before marriage; now paternity tests have eliminated that risk. Contraceptives have helped women's emancipation which means that, as Laura and Domenica did, we can also choose with whom we want to go to bed. Those are decisions only men could make before, the way Iliescu has been brought up. A normal person," and she again made the gesture signifying quotation marks, "might have rejected the girls, a macho type would have despised them and maybe called them whores, but he would have never murdered them. We face a clinical case, a disturbed personality."

"Sub-Inspector, would you say that the presumed behavior of Iliescu bears a relationship with gender violence?" Lluc asked.

"In a way he is punishing the girls because he thinks they are guilty," Manuela Vázquez responded, "and by punishing them he feels superior and powerful. He believes he's carrying out a justice that comes from God or from the Holy Ghost. Whatever. The husbands and lovers who kill their spouses also feel superior at the moment of killing; they prove to themselves that the victim has an identity only as a dominated person."

Lluçanès wanted to be heard and interrupted her: "But, leaving all those things aside, a person brought up with an iron fist, growing up in an orphanage, who had to struggle hard to become a university student with a sense of morality based on hard work, the contrast with our consumerist world, with our ethical laxity...'

But the inspector did not allow him to finish his speech. He realized his conclusion was enormously trivial and changed the topic: "Thank you, Sub-Inspector," he said. "I hope the nightmare is over, or almost...if the case against Iliescu holds. We know the salesgirl has not identified him and, of course, he denies everything. We need to verify from the airline that he did indeed take the flight to London and explain to us why they didn't alert us that his name was on the passenger list when the Sants men asked. And he will have to prove that on the days of the other murders, he was indeed in England, that he didn't go there and come back, that his van remained all the time in the airport parking lot. Of course, the forensic lab folks assure us that there is no trace of Laura or anything suspicious anywhere in the vehicle. Still, his lawyer will have to work hard during the next seventy-two hours if he does not want the judge to remand Iliescu to jail.

46

Constantinu Iliescu could prove that in the wee hours of Sunday, 7th December, the day of the second murder, he was at his friend Vasile Samoila's home in a South London neighborhood where many immigrants lived. Luckily for Iliescu, Vasile's wife celebrated her birthday that day and relatives and friends had filled the house and stayed till sunrise. They could all confirm that Iliescu had been with them all the time, eating *mititei* and *sarmale* that he himself had helped prepare the afternoon before the party.

As for Tuesday, 9th December, the day of the deaths of Bellpuig and Bru, Iliescu had been at the Tate Gallery. He didn't have an entrance ticket as the permanent exhibition was free, but he did have a ticket for the special exhibitions and had kept it. It was with the other papers in the folder inside his bag. Coincidentally, that very morning, he had thought of Laura Cremona when he'd noticed how much the girl looked like "The Lady of Shalott" in the painting by William Waterhouse. Yet it never occurred to him that Laura could have been murdered or that the same criminal had killed three other people, leaving the trademarks that appeared in some paintings by Flegel, those that Professor Bellpuig had shown the students.

Iliescu's alibi was air-tight and even though he had been the main suspect, there was no doubt that any judge would release him from custody after the seventy-two-hour limit. His lawyer had done an impeccable job. In less than twenty-four hours, he had gathered enough proof to exculpate his client; the police had no option but to yield to the evidence.

Lluçanès felt despondent and Manuela Vázquez even more so. She had been the chief engineer of the belief in Iliescu's guilt and had missed the mark. But she was sure of one thing: whoever had killed the professor and the three students was someone who also knew Iliescu and meant to put those deaths on him. She then surmised that besides Bellpuig, the only one who could be familiar with Iliescu's essay on the paintings was the professor's assistant.

Corporal Lluc had been assigned to talk to Jaume Pocoví after Bellpuig's murder as part of the process of finding evidence from those closest to the professor, but nothing useful had emerged from that conversation. The assistant seemed quite shaken by the professor's death, not only because it endangered his position – he had been admitted to the university, thanks to the recommendation and the interest Bellpuig had shown in him – but also because his doctoral thesis on cathedral gargoyles was now in limbo. Without the direction and encouragement of the professor, Pocoví told Lluc, he felt disoriented. Besides, he had thought of Bellpuig as a father. It was a terrible blow that he didn't know how to bear, the second one in that ill-fated 2008, for he had also broken up with his girlfriend recently, a development that plunged him into a depression which the pills prescribed by his doctor could not alleviate. He said they actually made things worse; they gave him insomnia which had led to the gash on his head: he had failed to see a door.

Lluc found nothing strange in Pocoví's reactions. He wrote in his notebook that the assistant was a shy type who surely admired the professor, a sentiment not quite reciprocated by Bellpuig – or at least, that was what one surmised from the conversation the professor had with the sub-inspector as she had informed the corporal.

It was Lluc who now phoned Pocoví. He told him he wanted to ask a couple of questions about a student who seemed suspicious and summoned him to the Egara Complex. He was ushered into the inspector's office there and was met by Lluçanès and Manuela Vázquez. It was an informal chat they assured him. They just wanted to know if he had graded the essays by the Erasmus students in Professor Bellpuig's class, if the comments on the papers were his.

Pocoví hesitated. He often graded exams and papers for Professor Bellpuig when he requested it, he told them, but that was not always the case. He couldn't remember if he had done it for those essays.

"Why do you want to know?" he asked, unable to hide his uneasiness. "What importance could that have?"

"There could be a clue in the exercises from the Erasmus students and we thought that if you graded them and can remember…"

Pocoví shook his head, but said nothing. He was a tall and burly man with a scruffy air. Some inept doctor had placed seven stitches on the right side of his head fairly recently as the scar was still pink. He was poorly dressed, had not shaved and his clothes were stained. According to his identity card, he was twenty-five, but seemed older. Manuela Vázquez noticed that his hands were sweating which made him rub them on his blue jeans.

Lluçanès exchanged glances with the sub-inspector who got up and walked to the door.

"The Sub-Inspector will bring us the essays," he said, "and you will be able to tell us if you graded them. Did you know the Erasmus students?"

"I did not."

"Had you never taught a class for them?"

"Only once or twice. The school was occupied and classes…" Pocoví went quiet and stared at the floor for a good while. Lluçanès realized something was not quite right with the assistant's brain, that his depression was stronger than Lluc had reported.

"Are you all right?" Lluçanès asked him and got up to go nearer him.

But Pocoví remained in his catatonic state, not moving a muscle, as if he hadn't heard. Neither did he answer Manuela

Vázquez who had just come back in with the folder and asked if he was OK. Only when they offered him a cup of coffee or some water, did he reply.

"Water, please," he uttered at last as though he had just returned from very far away and added: "I'm taking some medication that makes me very thirsty."

"You're not feeling well?" Lluçanès asked, sitting again behind his desk and pressing an intercom button to request a bottle of water.

"Makes sense," the sub-inspector said with a smile. "No professor from the Autònoma can feel normal after what happened and you least of all. Your students get killed, your professor gets killed..." As she said this, she pulled the essays by the students from the folder and set aside those that had some hand-written comment. After she had gathered these, she showed them to Pocoví.

"Is this your handwriting?"

The assistant glanced at them, still rubbing his hands on his thighs and answered in the affirmative.

"Did any of these exercises call your attention in particular?"

"I can't remember. No. You know, I've been going through a difficult time and haven't devoted myself to university work as I should have. I separated from my girlfriend thirty-seven days ago." He went silent and gulped the water that Lluçanès's secretary had just brought in.

"Bellpuig told us," the sub-inspector said.

"Really? Why did he tell you such thing?" Pocoví seemed suddenly interested.

"To excuse you, I imagine, since you didn't work enough lately," Lluçanès answered. "He also told us that he had decided against the renewal of your contract, that his report would be negative. Did you know that?"

Pocoví was quiet.

"Did you know? Had he told you? Answer!"

Lluçanès voice was stern, but the man seemed deeply troubled and did not speak. Suddenly, in a fit, he rose from his chair and ran to the door, sobbing.

Lluçanès went to him and grabbed his arm to prevent him from leaving.

"Sit down," he commanded, "and answer my question."

The assistant sat down, but said nothing and covered his face.

"Inspector," Manuela Vázquez said, "bear in mind that Senor Pocoví has suffered great trauma. It's normal for him not to be in any condition to answer. I think he is ruing all he's done."

Pocoví's sobs became louder. Then he began to squeal like a pig when it senses it's about to be slaughtered.

47

The warrant to arrest Pocoví had reached the inspector's office before the arrival of the assistant, but Lluçanès decided not to reveal its existence at first. Pocoví would be detained only if they really thought he was guilty. They couldn't allow themselves to make another mistake.

The media was in a frenzy over the error of Iliescu's detention and blamed a supposed xenophobia on the part of the Mossos d'Esquadra. They assumed that the clues that had led them to believe Iliescu was guilty had to do mostly with his being an immigrant from Eastern Europe and not with the facts the police thought implicated him. It wasn't the first time something like this had happened.

Even though Lluçanès had tried to prevent the information from reaching the press, the papers and news programs were portraying the mossos in a bad light. They were now a joke with the huge spectacle they had mounted on the motorway. They had behaved like extras in a second-rate American TV show. They were lucky for the good offices of the Romanian consul who advised Iliescu not to grant interviews and asked him to be discreet and show some understanding of the devastating situation. To keep Iliescu from temptation, the consul had him stay in his house. Iliescu, being shy, had no problem accepting Dimitri Vasilescu's suggestions; he did not want to feed any flames against the Mossos d'Esquadra either, preferring to have them on his side.

To both Lluçanès and Manuela Vázquez, working under so much pressure felt increasingly like an uphill battle. On the one hand, they had to arrest the suspects as soon as possible. They knew that only when they had the criminal in custody could calm return to Catalan society which had experienced a horror like never before. Not even the excitement provoked by the contract Barcelona's football club signed with Pep Guardiola as coach could compensate for the general sense of dread affecting all social exchanges. On the other hand, they would by no means allow themselves another error. They had to prove to the whole country that they were good for something beyond arresting pickpockets or writing up reports after traffic accidents, that they were an integral and necessary part of the social body at the service of the citizens as the interior minister, happy to have the mossos corps under his jurisdiction, had proudly proclaimed. But the minister was in a foul mood, having been questioned by opposition parties about his surprise proposal regarding police responsibilities and jurisdiction. This had led him to yell at the director-general, who, in turn, had called Lluçanès incompetent and remarked that the Policía Nacional, the police of the Spanish state, would have already arrested the murderer by then.

The inspector then passed the blame to the sub-inspector, who was trying to stay afloat. She had been most insistent in maintaining that Constantinu Iliescu was the main suspect and had taken the investigation in that direction, confident she wasn't wrong. This was why she now refused to trust her intuition and held onto the fact that the graphologists considered the handwriting of the voiceless woman compatible with that of the comments on Professor Bellpuig's exercises and now they knew that Pocoví had written those comments. He was left-handed to boot. As soon as he came to the inspector's office, the secretary had asked him to fill out a short form with his address and phone number, a routine request, she told him, no big deal. This allowed them to check if the assistant wrote with his left hand. According to the examiner, the blows that had killed both Bellpuig and Bru had been delivered by a leftie. Iliescu wrote with his right hand. The salesgirl from the mall at L'Illa, as she described a tall and strong man with sad eyes who wanted to purchase a plastic worm, had mentioned he took down the store's phone number with his left hand. If she could identify him, the sub-inspector was sure to have gotten it right this time.

Manuela Vázquez felt good about the decision Lluçanès had reached. She called Rifà on her cell and ordered him to locate the salesgirl immediately and bring her as fast as he could to look at Pocoví, as she had done when Iliescu was in custody. The agent went from Sabadell to Barcelona and back in record time. Someday, he might have a street named after him in his home town.

Montserrat Planes i Garriga was nervous. She would have never imagined that something like this would happen to her, that working in a store selling tchotchkes would lead her to be the one to identify the Autònoma's Assassin.

"If it weren't because you assure me of this," she told Rifà, "I would never believe that the guy who wanted those worms is not a good person."

The salesgirl had no doubt this time when it came to identifying Jaume Pocoví as her customer. She remembered his features well. Even though today he wasn't wearing a cap, he had on the same dark jacket as on the day he came to the store to ask if they had any plastic worms.

At this point, Lluçanès showed Jaume Pocoví the warrant, asked him if he wanted to give the name of a lawyer and told him he could make a phone call.

The assistant declined both offers. He had no one to call. "My girlfriend," he said, "hangs up when she hears my voice. And I don't know any lawyers."

48

The court-appointed lawyer was a young woman who had been given the case of a presumed murderer for the first time in her career and she vowed to Pocoví that she would defend him with all her might; he should trust her and tell her the truth. But the distracted man assured her he was indifferent to what might befall him and admitted he had killed Bellpuig because he was fed up with the professor's humiliations. He complained that he had to be on call any time of day or night to make photocopies, find books in the library or be given a class to teach at the last minute, and to top it all Bellpuig never appreciated his services and wanted to oust him from the university by denying him the assistantship.

He had killed Bellpuig and before that the two Erasmus students and Bru after. He explained those deaths as collateral damage. If he also murdered the students, it would be difficult for the police to think of a suspect who only wanted to kill the professor. The other deaths were part of his cover. Iliescu's disappearance served as his point of departure. He remembered the Romanian's essay very well. He himself had prepared the slides on Flegel for Bellpuig. Flegel was right: near the fruit, the flowers, the savory foods, the tastiest of fish, there was always present, whether we noticed it or not, a deadly element. Iliescu had seen this perfectly: a mouse, a cockroach, a fly, a worm. It had been easy to find the mouse, the cockroach and the fly. They belonged to his girlfriend's son. When she had kicked Pocoví out of her place, she had returned all that he'd ever given them, even the toys he'd bought for her son;

everything – as if she wanted to erase all traces down to the smallest ones – of his presence in her life and in her son's. The worm he had photocopied from a reproduction of the painting before; however, he had tried to find a plastic one like those he had used, but he had been told he'd have to order many, like a hundred and he didn't intend to kill so many people – those four were enough.

He had seen Laura on television and waited for her. He knew where she lived because he had also rented an apartment at the Vila, not in the same building but in a newer one. He had just moved in, not even a month before, after Anna had kicked him out of the house they shared near the Bellaterra train station. That was after she had gone to bed with Professor Bellpuig and become his lover. Pocoví waited for Laura that night in his car; she would show up sooner or later. He could wait. He suffered from insomnia. About two o' clock in the morning he saw Bru dropping her off at the corner of her building and went to the gate and spoke to her. "Why don't you come with me to Zona Hermètica for a night cap if you don't mind?" he asked her and added, "I've left my house because I couldn't sleep." She accepted, but thought she'd tell her roommate in case she felt like joining them if still awake. Laura told him to go up with her. They got to the apartment and went in without making any noise. From the doorknob in Domenica's bedroom hung a "DO NOT DISTURB" sign, but the door was ajar and they heard the people inside chatting. Pocoví recognized Bellpuig's voice perfectly. Some coincidence! "I knew he liked all types of women, but I did not suspect that just as he had stolen my girlfriend..." He was sure. It was the professor's voice. At other times, he thought he'd heard it only to realize he was confused and Bellpuig was not anywhere near him. He'd heard the voice in his own head. Not this time.

Pocoví stated all these facts coldly with great calm, with no show of distress. But after his reference to the voices, he went quiet for a long while, as though recalling that detail which was preventing him from going on. The lawyer had to pull him out of that almost catatonic state by repeatedly asking him what they did afterwards, where they went for their drinks, whether they left the campus area or not. Had he killed Laura in his car or somewhere else?

"I talked Laura into having the drink at my place. I had taped the interview; she might be eager to see herself and, as she watched, I prepared her a caipiroska. To put her to sleep I diluted two lorazepams in it. I think she was already quite drunk because she fell asleep immediately on the couch. The rest was easy. I used her own muffler; she hadn't taken it off. I was tired. I was also sleepy, but I couldn't go to sleep. I had to finish what I had started. I inserted the mouse into her vagina; it wasn't hard, just a small cut. Then I brought her down to my car and stuffed her into the trunk. The next day, I found a spot to hide her near the path that leads from the School of Letters to Ciutat Badia. I know the path well because I walked it daily when I was a student. I went to a place where there are some abandoned huts and a crazy person there threw a stone at me," he pointed at the gash on his head. "He told me he was the owner of all that and the King of Mambo and I had to go away. The doctor on call at the Sabadell clinic gave me this present," he pointed at the stitches.

He went on for the dazed lawyer's benefit: "That night I hid Laura in a crevice. I got there from the Letters parking lot with little difficulty. I kept Laura's bag which had the apartment's keys. That would make things easy for me. I imagined Bellpuig would return and then I…"

He went quiet again and stared at the floor. The lawyer waited for him to continue, but as he was not saying anything, she asked him: "Do you still have Laura's bag? The keys?"

"The bag, yes. I have it at home. I lost the keys."

Then, as if recalling the keys had prodded his memory, he proceeded: "The following Friday night I returned to Laura's apartment and got in using the key. Bellpuig was there. The voice coming from the bedroom was his. I got scared and decided to wait for him to fall asleep. I waited on the landing, but had to leave because some kids were walking up. I decided to wait for a couple of hours and then went home. I returned around four o' clock, and realized I didn't have the keys; they must have fallen off without my noticing, so I broke the lock open. It was easy to do; I always have a Swiss-Army knife with me. Bellpuig wasn't there this time. Domenica was alone, asleep in her bed. She hadn't removed her scarf. Perhaps she had a sore throat which made things easy for me. I squeezed hard..."

The lawyer couldn't repress a gesture of repulsion. She looked at the guy in front of her. He seemed like a lost soul, a good person. How could he have done that?

"Didn't you feel sorry for Domenica?"

"She was a whore like all of them."

"Don't say that. I think you have a rather poor opinion of women and it's just your luck to have a woman to defend you."

"I don't need anybody to defend me. I don't care what happens to me."

"You don't care if you go to prison?"

"I won't go to prison. I can assure you of that."

"It will be very hard to defend you if you show no remorse," the lawyer told him, "although I believe you are ill."

"True," he said, "I've been ill for a long time since the chickens' gas..."

"The chickens' gas? I don't know what you are talking about." This time the lawyer had to repress her laughter.

"The chickens' gas killed my whole family except for me. You know why? Because Bellpuig ordered me not to leave Barcelona so I could finish the job he had charged me with: to revise the proofs of one of his books. Little did he care that my grandmother's ninetieth birthday was coming up during the weekend he had ordered me to work.

"Tell me what happened."

"My mother had the idea of renting a country house for all of us to have a reunion and celebrate granny's ninetieth birthday. They all attended, my parents, my sisters, uncles, aunts, cousins, grandmother. Not me. I was grounded by my teacher. Too bad, come on, you have homework in Barcelona...It was a cold weekend, it was December like now and to keep warm, they turned on some heaters like those used in chicken farms that the owners had stored in the attic. The defective combustion killed them."

"I'm very sorry, believe me. Now that you mention it, it rings a bell…I understand that something like this…"

"The newspapers carried the news. You might have read it. The day I killed Bellpuig was exactly three years after the death of my folks. If I had been with them, if Bellpuig had not prevented me, I am sure they'd still be alive. I wouldn't have let them go to sleep with windows closed and the heaters on. It was he, the bastard, who was responsible!"

49

During her university years, Manuela Vázquez developed a special interest in schizophrenia, a mental illness that often appeared during adolescence and required strict vigilance, for it could become dangerous if not diagnosed in time. The textbooks and studies she had perused all showed the same basic features found in schizophrenics and those which, depending on the stages of the disease, could be easily identified. Pocoví's unkempt appearance, his mechanical gestures and long silences during which he seemed submerged in a void made her suspect the man was indeed schizophrenic. A high percentage of murderers suffered from the disease – the rest belonged to the group of psychopaths – and this was a point lawyers resorted to in their defense, as Pocoví's lawyer, Mercè Frontera, was doing. Frontera engaged the help of a psychiatrist who diagnosed Pocoví as suffering from impaired faculties and intense psychotic disturbances besides schizophrenia.

Despite all this, neither the other assistants nor the students at the school had ever suspected that the devoted aide to Bellpuig was affected by a mental illness. They saw him rather as a shy and introverted young man, incapable of reacting to the jokes and abuse from his professor who, a few times in public, had ordered Pocoví to tie his shoes and he had complied.

Just a few of the professors remembered Pocoví's family's tragedy since it had happened when he was in his third year at university and being a very good student, he had already been asked to help Bellpuig and been promised an assistantship. But no one at the Autònoma would have imagined that the last straw to drive him mad would be the affair between Bellpuig and Pocoví's girlfriend of two years, Anna Estrany, a nurse at the Bellvitge Hospital and the single mother of a three-year-old boy.

When Lluçanès summoned Pocoví's estranged girlfriend, she confirmed that the doctors had diagnosed him with schizophrenia early in 2008, but he had ignored their recommendations. He had recently stopped taking his medication. His temperament had changed drastically. He spent hours staring into space and had become distrustful and aggressive. He spied on her. He tried to listen in secretly on her telephone conversations and had even followed her on the street to find out where she was going which annoyed her no end. He had also lost all interest in his work. He often said he was on his way to the university and remained in bed doing nothing. He had abandoned the dissertation he'd been working on so industriously and spent hours staring at the ceiling. She didn't know how to get him out of a mess that seemed much worse than a strong depression. She had spoken to his doctors and got nothing; the two she consulted told her that if he didn't take his medication, he would never improve. She needed someone with authority to force him. Since Jaume had no relatives, she decided to go see Bellpuig. Surely, the professor would have noticed the change. He knew to what extreme Jaume admired him. He would obey and take his medicine if the professor ordered him to.

Bellpuig was most kind, invited her to lunch, told her that from that moment on, he would always be on her side, that, in effect, poor Jaume was not doing well at all, that they had to help him. But he also insisted that the young man wasn't good enough for her. She needed someone well balanced and strong and also someone who'd understand her and protect her.

At that point in Anna Estrany's narrative, her voice broke and her chin began to tremble, but she controlled her tears. Lluçanès looked at her and said nothing. He waited for her to go on, even though it was not difficult to imagine the rest of the story. Anna was tall, blonde, with deep eyes, very attractive. In a way, she reminded the inspector of Domenica. Obviously,

Bellpuig had set his eye on that type of woman. Anna tried to calm down and continued after a pause.

"We made love that very week in a room at the Serhs and kept meeting there. We had fallen in love; well, he maybe just a little, but I very much so. I loved him. I confessed the truth to Jaume – I did not want to lie to him – and asked him to leave my house, told him that our life together was over. I see now I was too hard on him; that was the worst thing one could do to someone who's ill. But we only live once and I wasn't ready to give up Bellpuig or become an adulterer. When things end, they end. We cannot do anything about it. Then Jaume threatened me. He said if I left him, he'd kill me and then kill himself, but at last, he went and left me alone. He'd call me from time to time…'

Anna Estrany paused. She opened her bag and got out a box of lozenges. She offered one to the inspector and took one for herself before proceeding.

"You know, Inspector? I wonder whether in some way, I am guilty for all that's happened. Unwittingly, of course. If I hadn't confessed to Jaume, if he hadn't learnt that Bellpuig and I…. If I hadn't kicked him out, if I had lied, Jaume would not have killed anyone. The truth is always a luxury; Carles used to say and now I think he was right. He preferred to keep our relationship private, clandestine and was against my telling everything to Jaume. 'It might be counterproductive in his state,' he had warned, but I never imagined Jaume would be driven to the point of killing four people. Now that I have thought about it a lot, I've reached the conclusion that there was another reason for me to continue lying. If Bellpuig knew that our affair – which I believed would last forever – would be short-lived, then it didn't make sense, given the way he saw things, for me to stop being his assistant's girlfriend. My cuckolding Jaume was a detail of no importance; Bellpuig could see things as his right…what did the feudal lords have? Yes, his *droit du seigneur.*"

Josep Lluçanès considered what Anna was saying and even though his work consisted in great measure of looking for the truth, he admitted that often in life, to carry on, one needed to resort to the benefit of lies. Without lies everything would be more difficult. But he kept such reflection to himself and returned to what he wanted to ask.

"Did you meet Bellpuig at the hotel the night of Friday 28th to Saturday 29th?"

"I called Carles to tell him I wouldn't be there, that I couldn't leave home; my son had a fever. I imagine he didn't appreciate being stood up and therefore punished me. He refused to meet me on the following Friday. Yet, on the evening of 5th December, I phoned the hotel. I had a notion that he'd be there, waiting for me…he answered from a room and asked me not to go there because he wasn't alone. Suddenly I felt the earth was sinking under me. I kept calling, but no one answered from the room or from his cell. I did not understand anything. Not wanting to lose my dignity entirely, I stopped calling him. Yet I expected he'd call me or come by to explain what had happened, but he didn't do so during the whole weekend. The last thing I knew was that he had died, that someone had killed him."

Her chin was trembling again and she covered her face with her hands. The inspector thought Anna Estrany quite attractive. He was gawking at her long, shapely legs. The luck of that poor wretch, Pocovíto, be living with her! He waited a few seconds before he went on to ask his questions.

"Did it ever occur to you that it could have been Jaume?"

"It never did, I swear. I would have never imagined it. Despite how angry he was that I had fallen for Carles, he was threatening me, not him. He worshipped his teacher even though Bellpuig despised him and used him, as he did me, as he probably used everyone. To dump me without a word, with no explanation whatsoever…"

Lluçanès felt tempted to say that he didn't understand how Bellpuig could have preferred Domenica to her. The woman in front of him seemed more mature, more grown up, more intelligent, and she was gorgeous. Besides, she was in love with the professor. At that instant, he had a thought; precisely because Anna was in love with Bellpuig, he wanted to flee from her and Domenica became the excuse. As he remembered Domenica, the inspector realized the name Bellpuig had used for Anna was Mònica. Both names ended with the same letter.

"He talked to us about you, but called you Mònica," he told her. Then he added a white lie: "He told us you were the woman for him and that he loved you. Domenica was an adventure of no importance. He refused to give us your real name in order to protect you. Did he ever call you Mònica instead of Anna?"

Anna opened her eyes very wide before answering.

"Mònica? No, never. He liked the name Anna a lot, it was his mother's name also."

50

Sub-Inspector Manuela Vázquez thought that she should inform the dean and the Erasmus students' adviser before the midday news revealed that Jaume Pocoví, having confessed to the four crimes, had been jailed. One could say the two women had worked side by side with the mossos. They deserved the courtesy, especially Rosa Casasaies, whom the sub-inspector considered a friend. Not so much Dolors Adrover. Despite her position as dean, Manuela had dealt less with her. Even though she was still on leave, Rosa had agreed to go to the campus to meet Manuela Vázquez.

Seated at the table in the dean's meeting room in her street clothes – the same olive-green Zara jacket and gray trousers she had been wearing when she had spoken with Rosa Casasaies and poor Domenica for the first time – the sub-inspector explained that there was no doubt that Jaume Pocoví, an assistant in the Department of Art, had killed Laura Cremona, Domenica Arrigo, Marcel Bru and Carles Bellpuig. She told them what the motive of the crimes had been according to the accused. She insisted that as she understood things, it was a case of a mentally ill person who might be better off finding no cure because if he did, he would probably become conscious of what he had done and would be incapable of accepting his error.

As Manuela spoke, Rosa Casasaies could not contain her tears, hard as she tried. She felt pity for the assistant; the poor unfortunate would be sent to a penitentiary hospital for many years, but she felt deeper compassion for the four dead. She thought especially of the lives of the three students cut short, sacrificed solely, as the inspector revealed, to mask Pocoví's true intentions. Despite being despotic, a philanderer and a liar, Bellpuig did not deserve such an ending either. If he got to be that way, it was because the rest of people let him, even she…No one had stood up to him.

Rosa Casasaies could still hear the young voices in that room: Laura Cremona sounded irate, Domenica Arrigo sounded like a flock of chirping birds and the most insolent voice was poor Bru's whom she had so disliked…Again she put herself in their parent's shoes and pitied them too. For a brief moment, she felt immensely relieved that nothing had happened to her own daughter. She could understand the obstinate rancor of Marcel Bru's mother who kept blaming the police, first for having considered her son a suspect and then for having failed to protect him. She had asked for a public explanation from the minister of the interior and the president of the Generalitat. Pocoví's parents were fortunate to be no longer in this world because they didn't have to suffer the horror of seeing their son imprisoned and accused.

All that had happened during that miserable December had distressed Rosa Casasaies and she could not stop reliving the events. Her husband told her that it was normal, that it would be weird if she felt indifferent to the tragedy that had befallen the Autònoma and affected her so deeply and assured her she would slowly recover her calm. To give her some serenity, he was taking her to spend the holidays in Vienna with Cristina. They would try to fulfill one of Rosa's wishes: to attend the New Year's concert there. It was extremely difficult to find tickets, even more so this last minute, but he knew the conductor of the Wiener Musikverein because they had been together on the tribunal for a master's degree in musical psychology, and the musician had promised to try and get tickets for him. If he managed that, the happy memory of having clapped in time for the Radetzky March played by the Vienna Philharmonic would help Rosa overcome the sad memories and she would usher in 2009 on a good note.

On the other hand, the antidepressants and tranquilizers the dean was taking and the constant conversations in Latin with her dead husband made her less vulnerable to dramatics or perhaps just prevented its expression. Still, she was quite distressed. The fact that the murderer was from the Department of Art History in the same school was one more negative element to add to all other negative elements of that frightful year, the worst of her deanship tenure. But she gave vent to her disquiet less than Rosa Casasaies, even though she had lost eight kilograms since the anti-Bologna occupation had started. The occupiers, luckily for her, had left the campus without the need for force. For the time being, with the holiday break about to start and no classes being held at the school, it didn't seem likely that they would return.

Manuela Vázquez was right: the university could breathe easy at last; there would be no more murders. There was no doubt now. Jaume Pocoví had confessed. There was also objective evidence against him. The mossos working on the case had found in the apartment Pocoví had rented at the Vila, Laura's bag and the woman's outfit and wig he used to disguise himself when he went to the campus to murder Bellpuig. Rosario Hurtado recognized them at once. In Pocoví's car trunk, besides a bunch of fingerprints, they found one of Laura's shoes with very high stiletto heels, part of the wardrobe with which the poor girl had dreamed of conquering the world.

9 781783 084616